THE ENIGMA
OF THE RETURN

Dany Laferrière

THE ENIGMA
OF THE RETURN

Translated from the French by
David Homel

MACLEHOSE PRESS
QUERCUS · LONDON

First published in the French language as *L'énigme du retour*
by Éditions Grasset et Fasquelle, Paris, 2009
First published in English by Douglas & McIntyre, Vancouver, 2011
First published in Great Britain by

MacLehose Press
an imprint of Quercus
55 Baker Street
7th Floor, South Block
London W1U 8EW

A CIP catalogue record for this book is available
from the British Library

ISBN (TPB) 978 0 85705 048 9
ISBN (Ebook) 978 0 85738 436 2

10 9 8 7 6 5 4 3 2 1

Printed and bound in the UK by Clays Plc, St Ives Ltd

At the end of daybreak . . .

AIMÉ CÉSAIRE

Notebook of a Return to the Native Land, 1939

To Dany Charles, my nephew,
who lives in Port-au-Prince

PART ONE

Slow Preparations for Departure

The Phone Call

The news cuts the night in two.
The inevitable phone call
that every middle-aged man
one day will receive.
My father has died.

I got on the road early this morning.
No destination.
The way my life will be from now on.

I stop along the way for breakfast.
Bacon and eggs, toast, scalding hot coffee.
I sit by the window.
A sharp sun warms my right cheek.
A quick glance at the paper.
A bloody image of a car wreck.
Death is sold anonymously in America.

I watch the waitress moving
among the tables.
Busy with her rounds.
The nape of her neck is sweaty.

The radio is playing this country song,
the story of a cowboy
unhappy in love.
The waitress has a red flower tattooed
on her right shoulder.
She turns and gives me a sad smile.

I leave the tip on the newspaper
next to the cup of cold coffee.
Walking toward the car I try to imagine
the loneliness of a man facing death
in a hospital bed in a foreign country.

"Death expires in a white pool of silence,"
wrote the young Martinican poet Aimé Césaire
in 1939.
What can anyone know of exile and death
when they're not even twenty-five?

I get back on Highway 40.
Little villages numb with sleep
along the frozen river.
Where are they all hiding?
The invisible people.

The feeling of discovering
virgin territory.
For no good reason I take
a country road
that will set me back by an hour.

A vast land of ice.
It's difficult for me
even after so many years
to imagine the shape
next summer will take.

Ice burns
more fiercely
than fire
but the grass remembers
the caress of the sun.

There are, beneath this ice,
hotter desires
and sharper impulses
than in any other season.
The women here know it.

The men sweat for a living and
the first to open his mouth is a sissy.
Silence is the rule of the forest
if you don't want to be surprised by a bear.

He nurtured silence so long
that emptiness took hold of him.
The man became a dry branch
that cracked in the cold.

Hunger brings the wolf out of the woods
and drives the woodsman home.
He nods off, after his bowl of soup,
by the fireplace.
His wife tells him what they said on the radio.
It's always about war and lost jobs.
So go the centuries in these northern villages.

It's easy to talk when we're warm,
and binding old wounds.
The wounds we're ashamed of
never heal.

I always panic when
I can't hear another human sound.
I am a creature of the city.
My rhythm is the staccato heels
of a woman coming up behind me.

I have lost all direction.
Snow has covered everything.
Ice has burned away the smells.
The realm of winter.
Only a native can find his way through this.

A big bright yellow truck roars past.
The driver, happy to finally
meet someone on the road,
blows his horn wildly.
He's heading south.
I'm driving into the luminous north
that blinds and enchants me.

I know at the end of this road
a bearded man full of gentle fury,
surrounded by a pack of dogs,
is trying to write the great American novel.

Hunkered down in the sleeping village of Trois-Pistoles
on the edge of the frozen river,
he is the only one today who knows how
to dance with ghosts, madmen and the dead.

This bluish light
sweeping the river
swallows me up in a single breath.
The car begins to skid.
I recover just in time.
To die amid beauty
is not granted to the petit bourgeois man
that I am.

I am aware of being in a world
completely different from my own.
The fire of the South crossing
the ice of the North
produces a temperate sea of tears.

When the road is straight like this,
ice on both sides,
no clouds to help
me find my way under the noonday sky
so completely blue,
I can touch infinity.

I really am among those northern people
who drink till they go mad
dancing a broken jig.
They scream obscenities at the sky
and are astonished to find themselves alone
on a giant sheet of ice.

The feeling of driving
through one of those
cheap paintings hanging
above the fireplace.
Landscape within the landscape.

At the far end of the dirt road,
her feet not touching the ground,
that little girl with the black hair
and the fever-colored yellow dress is dancing.
The one who has lived in my dreams
since the summer I was ten.

A quick glance at the gauges
to see how much gasoline is left.
A breakdown on this road
means certain death.
Magnanimous, the cold numbs before it kills.

The dogs are fighting under the table.
The cats playing with their shadows.
The old goat grazing on the carpet.
The master of the house has gone into the woods
for the day, the old housekeeper tells me.

I turn back as I go out the door
and see the cats tearing apart
a fat manuscript that has fallen from a shelf.
The housekeeper's indulgent smile seems to say
that here animals come before literature.

Returning to Montreal.
Tired.
I stop by the side of the road.
A quick nap in the car.

Childhood wells up behind closed eyelids.
I wander beneath the tropical sun
but it is cold as death.
The need to piss wakes me up.
A burning sensation before the liquid spurts out.

The same emotion every time
I see the city in the distance.
I take the tunnel under the river.
We always forget that Montreal is an island.

The low-angled light on the smokestacks
above the Pointe-aux-Trembles factories.
The melancholy headlights of the cars.
I make my way to the Cheval Blanc.

The afternoon drinkers have gone.
The late-night ones haven't shown up yet.
I love this brief moment
when no one is around.

The guy next to me is stretched out on the counter
mouth open and eyes half closed.
They serve me my usual glass of rum.
I think of a dead man whose features
have yet to come together in my mind.

On the Proper Use of Sleep

I got home late at night.
I ran myself a bath.
I always feel at home in water.
An aquatic animal—that's what I am.
Césaire's water-warped collection on the floor.
I dried my hands before reaching for it.

I fell asleep in the pink bathtub.
That old fatigue
whose cause I pretend not to know
carried me off
toward uncharted territories.

I slept for an eternity.
That was the only way
to return incognito to the country
with my momentous news.
The night horse that sometimes
I ride at noon knows the path
across the desolate savannah.

Galloping across the mournful plain of time
before discovering
that there is in this life
neither north nor south
father nor son
and that no one
really knows where to go.

We can build our dream house
on the slope of a mountain.
Paint the shutters nostalgia blue.
Plant oleander all around.
Then sit at twilight to watch
the sun sink so slowly into the gulf.
We can do that in each of our dreams
but we'll never recover the flavor
of those childhood afternoons spent
watching the rain fall.

I remember I would throw myself on the bed
to try to calm the hunger
that devoured me from within.
Today, I sleep
to leave my body
and quench my thirst for the faces of the past.

The little airplane passes steadily
through the great hourglass
that erases the tape of memory.
Here I stand before a new life.
Not everybody gets to be reborn.

I go around a corner in Montreal
and just like that
I find myself in Port-au-Prince.
Like in some teenage dream
where you're kissing a different girl than the one
you're holding in your arms.

To sleep and awake again in the country I left
one morning without looking back.
A long reverie made up of unrelated images.
Meanwhile the bathwater has grown cold
and I find I've developed gills.

This lethargy always hits me
this time of year
when winter has settled in
and spring is still so far away.
In the midst of the ice at the end of January
I have no more energy to continue
but it's impossible to turn back.

I've started to write again the way
some people start smoking.
Without admitting it to anyone.
And with that feeling I'm doing something
that's not good for me
but that I can't resist
any longer.

As soon as I open my mouth, vowels and consonants pour out in
a disorderly mess and I have stopped trying to control it. I disci-
pline myself enough to try writing, but after a dozen lines I stop
out of exhaustion. I need to find a way that doesn't demand too
much physical effort.

When I bought my old Remington 22, a quarter century ago,
I did it to adopt a new style. Tougher, more intense than before.
Writing by hand seemed too literary. I wanted to be a rock 'n'
roll writer. A writer of the machine age. Words interested me
less than the sound of the keyboard. I had energy to burn. In my

narrow room on Saint-Denis Street, I spent all day typing fever-
ishly in the dark. I worked, the windows closed, bare-chested in
summer's furnace-room. With a bottle of cheap wine at my feet.

I return to my trusty pen
which never lets me down.
At the end of a cycle of overwork
we always return to what seems
most natural.

After all these years
there is practically nothing spontaneous left in me.
Yet when the news was announced over the telephone
I heard that short dry click
that can make your heart stop.

A man accosted me in the street.
Are you still writing? Sometimes.
You said you weren't writing any more. That's true.
Then why are you writing now?
I don't know.
He went off, offended.

Most readers
see themselves as characters in a novel.
They consider their lives a tale
full of sound and fury
for which the writer should be
their humble scribe.

There is as much mystery in getting close
to a person as in moving apart.
Between those two points
stretches stifling daily life
with its string of petty secrets.

From which end will I take this day?
By the rising or the setting of the sun?
These days I've been getting up
when the sun is going down.

First I need a glass of rum
to dissipate the passion of malaria,
the fever I sometimes confuse
with the energy of life.
I won't fall asleep until the bottle
is lying on the wooden floor.

When I smile this way in the shadows
it's because I feel lost
and no one in that case
will make me leave
the pink bathtub
where I curl up in a ball,
a round belly filled with water.

Exile

This morning I picked up the first black notebook
that tells how I came to Montreal.
It was the summer of 1976.
I was twenty-three.
I had just left my country.
Thirty-three years living
far from my mother's eyes.

Between the journey and the return,
stuck in the middle,
this rotten time
can lead to madness.

That moment always comes
when you stop recognizing yourself
in the mirror.
You've lived too long without witnesses.

I compare myself to the photo
of the young man I was before the departure.
The photo my mother slipped
into my pocket just as I
closed the low green gate.
I remember all that sentimentality
made me smile back then.
Today that old photo is my only
reflection to measure passing time.

Sunday afternoon in Port-au-Prince.
I can tell because even the plants
look bored.
We are sitting, my mother and I,
on the gallery, in silence, waiting
for darkness to settle over the oleander.

In the yellowed photo
I am paging through
(no doubt with moist palms and pounding heart)
the summer issue of a woman's magazine
with girls in bikinis.
Next to me, my mother pretends to sleep.

If I didn't know then that
I was going to leave
and never return,
my mother, so careworn
that day,
must have felt it
in the most secret part
of her body.

We're stuck in a bad novel
ruled by a tropical dictator
who keeps ordering
the beheading of his subjects.
We scarcely have time
to escape between the lines
toward the margin that borders the Caribbean Sea.

Here I am years later
in a snow-covered city
walking and thinking of nothing.
I am guided only
by the movements of frigid air
and that fragile neck ahead of me.

Intrigued by the strength
that girl has, so determined,
confronting the harsh
and frigid winds that bring
tears to my eyes
and whirl me around like a dervish.

A child sitting in the middle of the stairway
waits for his father to take him to the arena.
From his sad look I can see
that the game has already started.
I would have given anything
to miss a game
and spend the afternoon watching my father
read his paper in the corner café.

I know that house with a cat in the window.
To enter you have to put
the key in all the way
then draw it back as you turn it
gently in the lock.
The stairs begin to creak
at the eighth step.

A big wooden house.
A long bare table
with a basket of fruit at the end.
On the wall a display
of black-and-white photos
that tell the story
of a man and a woman
in the blaze of love.

A little squirrel climbs the tree at top speed
turning its head in my direction
as if inviting me to follow.
The pale light of three a.m.
when teenage girls walk the streets
on stiletto heels that will break their backs
before they reach thirty.

That girl in the green miniskirt and the cracked lips gets paid
at dawn in cocaine cut with baking soda just before the cops
come by then she sniffs the stuff right there to face the cold
stares of the proper ladies in purple curlers keeping an eye on
their brats from the window.

    It's rare that I'm in more of a hurry than a squirrel. But
that's the case today. The animal is amazed that this passerby
doesn't want to feed or play with it. No one's taught it that it's
just a poor squirrel living in an ordinary neighborhood park.
Social classes might not exist among animals. But ego does.

I wait for the café to open.
The waitress pulls up on her bike
despite the cold.
She grabs the two piles of papers
the young delivery boy left earlier
in front of the door.
I watch her go about her business behind the bay window.
Her movements are precise and driven by habit.
Finally she opens the door.

I go in for my first coffee and
read the morning's editorials
which always make me furious.
She puts on heavy metal at top volume
but she'll change it to Joan Baez
when the first customers show up.

I always stop in at the bookseller's next door. She's at her post
behind the counter. Her features are drawn. Winter is not kind
to her. She's about to go to Key West to see a writer friend who
has been living there for the past years. Literature, like organized crime, has its networks.

The reader's bent neck as he stands at the back.
His left profile.
Clenched jaw.
Intense concentration.
He's about to change centuries.
Right before my eyes.
Without a sound.

I always thought
that books crossed
the centuries to reach us.
Then I understood
seeing that man
the reader does the traveling.

Let us not trust too much in that object covered in signs
that we hold in our hands
and that is there only to attest
the journey really did take place.

I go back to the café next door. The waitress signals that
someone has been waiting for me. After Joan Baez, it's Native
singer Buffy Sainte-Marie's turn. I'd completely forgotten the
appointment. I beg to be pardoned. The young journalist asks
me coldly whether she can record our conversation. I tell her
yes, even though I know that the point of conversations is to
leave no trace. She works for one of those free weeklies that
litter the tables of the local cafés. T-shirt, jeans, tattoos,
roseate eyelids, sparkling eyes. I order a tomato salad. She
goes for a green salad. Sometime in the 1980s, we moved from
the culture of steak to the culture of salad in the hope it would
make us more peaceful.

   The machine records. So really, you're just writing about
identity? I write only about myself. You've already said that.
It doesn't seem to have been heard. Do you think people aren't
listening to you? People read in search of themselves and not
to discover someone else. Paranoid, perhaps? Not enough.
Do you think one day you'll be read for yourself? That was my
last illusion until I met you. You seem to me different in reality.
Why, have we met in a book before? She gathers up her material
with that bored look that can ruin even a sunny day.

The only place I feel completely at home is in this scalding water that warms my bones. The bottle of rum within reach, never too far from Césaire's collection of poems. I alternate mouthfuls of rum and pages of the Notebook until the book slides onto the floor. Everything is happening in slow motion. In my dream, Césaire takes my father's place. The same faded smile and that way of crossing his legs that reminds me of the dandies of the postwar days.

I have studied that photo of my father for so long.
His well-starched shirt collar.
The mother-of-pearl cufflinks.
Silk socks and shined shoes.
The loose knot of his tie.
A revolutionary is above all a charmer.

The weatherman is calling for twenty-eight below this morning.
Hot tea.
I am reading by the frosted window.
Numbness fills me.
I lay the book on my stomach.
My hands together and my head thrown back.
Nothing else will happen today.

This sunbeam
that warms my left cheek.
A child's afternoon nap
not far from his mother.
In the shadow of the oleander.
Like an old lizard
hiding from the sun.

Suddenly I hear that dull sound
the book makes as it falls to the floor.
The same sound that
the heavy juicy mangos of my childhood made
as they fell by the water basin.
Everything brings me back to childhood.
That fatherless country.

What's for sure is that
I wouldn't have written this way had I stayed behind.
Maybe I wouldn't have written at all.
Far from our country, do we write to console ourselves?
I have doubts about the vocation of the writer in exile.

The Photo

A man sitting in front of a thatched hut
with a peasant hat on his head.
A plume of smoke rising behind him.
"That's your father in the countryside,"
my mother said to me.
The President-for-Life's henchmen were looking for him.
Distant as it is,
that picture comforts me even today.

When it's noon and I'm too hot
in these *tristes tropiques*
I will remember my walk
on the frozen lake, near the cabin
where my friend Louise Warren
would go to write.

Cats play on the porch
without concern for passing time.
Their time is not ours.
This kitten slips
into the shadows of my memory.
White socks on the
waxed wood floor.

I've lost track of myself.
Memories run together in my mind.
My life is just a small damp package
of washed-out colors and old smells.

It's as if an eternity had passed
since the phone call.
Time is no longer cut
into fine slices called days.
It's become a compact mass with a density
greater than the earth's.

Nothing beyond this imperious need to sleep. Sleep is my only way of dodging the day and the obligations it brings. I have to admit that things have been falling apart for some time now. My father's death has completed a cycle. It all happened without my knowledge. I had just begun picking up the signs that warned of this maelstrom and already it was carrying me off.

Images from deep in childhood
wash over me like a wave
with such newness
I really feel I am seeing
the scene unfold before me.

I remember another detail
from that picture of my father
but so tiny that my mind
can't locate it.
All I can recall is the memory
of a moment of pleasure.

I remember now what made me laugh so much when my mother showed me the photo of the peasant in the straw hat. I was six years old. In the left corner, a chicken was scratching at the ground. My mother wondered what I thought was so funny about a chicken. I couldn't explain what I felt. Today I know: a chicken is so alive it moves even in a picture. Compared to the chicken, everything else looks dead. For me, my father's face can't begin to move without my mother's voice.

The Right Moment

This moment always comes.
When it's time to leave.
We can always hang around a little,
say useless goodbyes and gather up
things we'll abandon along the way.
The moment stares at us
and we know it won't back down.

The moment of departure awaits us by the door.
Like something whose presence we feel
but can't touch.
In reality, it takes on the form of a suitcase.

Time spent anywhere else than
in our native village
is time that cannot be measured.
Time out of time written
in our genes.

Only a mother can keep that sort of count.
For thirty-three years
on an Esso calendar
mine drew a cross over each day
spent without seeing me.

If I meet my neighbor on the sidewalk
he never fails to invite me in
to taste the wine he makes in his basement.
We spend the afternoon discussing Juventus
back in the days when Juventus was Juventus.
He personally knows all the players
though most have been dead for some time.

I ask Garibaldi (I call him that because he worships Garibaldi) why he doesn't go back to his country. Mine, I say, is so devastated that it hurts just thinking about seeing it again. But you, just to go back to the stadium to watch Juventus play. He takes the time to go and shut off the television then returns to sit near me. He looks me in the eye and tells me he goes back to Italy every night.

Garibaldi invites me to his place one evening. We go down to the basement. The same ritual. I have to drink his homemade wine. I feel he has something important to tell me. I wait. He gets up, wipes the dust off his books, then produces a signed portrait of D'Annunzio that the writer dedicated to his father. I'm afraid he's going to entrust me with some scandalous confession. But he just needed to tell me that he's always hated Juventus, and that his team is Torino fc. Since no one knows that team here and everyone knows Juventus, he says Juventus thinking of Torino. That's the tragedy of his life. Not a day goes by when he doesn't think of that betrayal. If one day he ever returns to Italy he isn't sure he'll be able to look his old friends in the eye.

I bring back to the country
without a farewell ceremony
these gods who accompanied me
on this long journey
and kept me from losing my mind.
If you don't know voodoo,
voodoo knows you.

The faces I once loved disappear
with the days of our burned memory.
The sheer fact of not recognizing
even those who were close to us.
The grass grows in, after the fire,
to camouflage all trace of the disaster.

In fact, the real opposition is not
between countries, no matter how different they are,
but between those who have had to learn
to live at other latitudes
(even in inferior conditions)
and those who have never had to face
a culture other than their own.

Only a journey without a return ticket
can save us from family, blood
and small-town thinking.
Those who have never left their village
live unchanging lives
that can prove, with time,
dangerous for their personality.

For three-quarters of the people on this planet
only one type of travel is possible
and that's to find themselves without papers
in a country whose language and customs
they know nothing of.

There's no sense accusing them
of wanting to change
other people's lives
when they have
no control
over their own.

If we really want to leave we have to forget
the very idea of the suitcase.
Things don't belong to us.
We accumulate them out of the simple need for comfort.
A comfort we have to question
before walking out the door.
We have to understand that the minimum level of comfort
needed to live here in winter
is a dream come true back there.

When I came here, I had one small suitcase into which I could
put everything. What I possess today is spread out through
my room. I wonder what happened to that first suitcase. Did I
forget it in a closet during a quick move? In those days I would
slip out, leaving the last month's rent on the table and a girl
sleeping in the bed.

　　Garibaldi just went by with his grandson, who comes to visit
him every Friday after school. He makes him pasta and talks
away to him in dialect. The boy is only ten years old, but when
you ask him who he hates most of all in the world, he tells you
Gianni Agnelli, the owner of Juventus. His son doesn't want
to hear anything about Italy; he likes hockey because it makes
him feel closer to the country where he was born. Garibaldi will
take revenge on his grandson who will inherit his bottles of bad
homemade wine and the yellowed portrait of D'Annunzio.

I fear that an event no matter how great
will never shake
a man from his habits.
The decision is made long before
we actually become aware of it
and for a reason that will always escape us.
The moment of departure has been written
in us so long ago that by the time it comes
it always seems a little banal.

Time in Books

As soon as I moved into a new apartment
I would place my books on the table.
All of them read and reread.
I wouldn't buy a book unless
the desire to read it was stronger
than the hunger in my belly.

That's still the case for a lot of people.
When our circumstances change
we think it's the same
for everyone else.
I know people who constantly
have to choose between eating and reading.

I consume as much meat here
in one winter
as a poor person in Haiti eats
in a lifetime.
I moved very quickly
from forced vegetarian to obligated carnivore.

In my life before, food
was a daily preoccupation.
Everything centered on my stomach.
Once I got something to eat everything was settled.
That's impossible to understand
if you've never experienced it.

Two years ago, after a violent hurricane struck Haiti, I received
a letter from a young student who urged me to inform all people
of good will who were thinking of sending food to the victims
that it would be better if every bag of rice was accompanied by
a case of books because, he wrote, "We do not eat to live, but to
be able to read."

One day, I bought a book
without really needing to.
It sat on the little kitchen table
unopened for three months
among the onions and carrots.
Today I realize that a good half
of my library remains unread.

I'm waiting to be in a sanatorium before I read Buddenbrooks
by the serious Thomas Mann, or track The Leopard by Giuseppe
Tomasi di Lampedusa. Why do we keep books we'll never read?
For The Leopard, the author's name justified the expense.
I forget what keeps me from reading Thomas Mann's novel.

I will leave with a little suitcase.
Like the one I had when I came here.
Nearly empty.
Not a single book.
Not even mine.

Stay only one short night in Port-au-Prince
before heading to Petit-Goâve to
see that house again not far
from my grandfather's old distillery.
Later I'll cross the rusty old bridge
to visit my grandmother in the cemetery.

I'd just as soon spend the rest of my time here
chatting about everything and nothing
with people who have never
opened a book in their lives.
But sooner or later that essential moment will come
when I confuse the novels I read
with the ones I wrote.

Everything moves on this planet.
Seen from the sky its southern flank
is in constant motion.
Entire populations travel northward
in search of life.
When everyone gets there
we'll all tip over the edge.

Sometimes a phone call in the middle of the night
turns everything upside down in an instant.
We are lost in restless movement.
It's always easier to change places
than change lives.

Into a suitcase I throw two or three pairs of jeans, three shirts,
two pairs of socks, some underwear, a tube of toothpaste,
two toothbrushes, a box of aspirin and my passport. I drink
a final glass of water in the middle of the kitchen before
switching off the lights for the last time.

In a Café

My head lowered into the frigid wind, I go to the corner.
I've walked this street for thirty years. I know every smell (the
Tonkinese soup with the strips of rare beef from the little
Vietnamese restaurant), every color (the graffiti on the walls
of the old hotel with rooms by the hour), every taste (the fruit
market where I buy apples in winter and mangos in summer)
along Saint-Denis. Clothing stores have replaced the used book-
stores. Indian, Thai and Chinese restaurants instead of crummy
bars where you could spend all day over a warm beer.

I slip into the student café
on the corner of Ontario Street.
The waitress looks my way and doesn't smile.
I sit at the back, by the radiator.
After a while she comes to take my order.
I can barely hear Arcade Fire.
A quick breakfast before heading to the station.

On the paper placemat I scribble down these quick notes
(with little drawings between each scene) for song ideas as
I sip my coffee.

side a

Scene 1: I wander the streets with the key to my room in my
pocket. I'm afraid of losing the key even as I savor the idea
(close at hand) that everything I own at this very moment is
in my pocket.

Scene 2: I meet a friend I knew in Port-au-Prince and he invites
me to his place. His wife welcomes me with bedroom eyes and
a smile that's too sensual. I don't stick around because I don't
play that game.

Scene 3: I go by the museum where the Modigliani show is on. I get in without paying. His life is no different from mine: frugal repasts, girls with long necks and cheap wine.

Scene 4: I'm sitting on a park bench, right across from the library. Right next to me two teenagers are kissing as a stunned squirrel looks on. The ducks are indifferent to the whole thing.

Scene 5: I'm making myself spaghetti with garlic sauce while keeping one eye on an old war film on my little black-and-white tv. It stars that German actress with the heavy hands—what is her name again?

Scene 6: From my window, I follow that girl in the summer dress (her legs and shoulders bare) all the way to her door. She turns around, feeling my eyes on the nape of her neck, then goes inside. Two days later, she is in my bathtub.

side b
Scene 7: A well-dressed lady is walking in front of me on Laurier Street. She drops an earring. I try and tell her. She pays me no attention. I thrust the earring in her face. She grabs it out of my hand. And looks at me as if I had tried to steal her jewelry.

Scene 8: In a bar, people are talking about suicide. I'm always impressed by the courage it takes to choose death that way. The guy next to me says he's already made two serious attempts, but he couldn't stand a single day of exile. It's the opposite for me. I don't think I could survive suicide.

Scene 9: I'm in Repentigny, a small, well-off suburban town. Kids are dreaming of showing their paintings in a Montreal art gallery some day. I advise them to start by showing their work in their living rooms. They're amazed they haven't thought of that before. I come from a country where we're used to making do with what we have.

Scene 10: A bunch of us are out together and the girl I've been sneaking looks at comes and kisses me. An endless kiss. Her boyfriend looks on with a smile. We haven't drunk or smoked anything. Her kiss sets off a small explosion in my brain—which completely changes my view of relations between men and women. In Port-au-Prince, a look would have done the trick.

Scene 11: I go to a resource center for immigrant workers on Sherbrooke Street. If you're really badly off, they'll give you twenty dollars to get through the day. We talk politics and the guy wants to know in what circumstances I left the country, and whether I'd been tortured. The answer is no. He insists, because just getting slapped in the face would have been worth 120 dollars. The answer is still no. As I leave the office he slips me an envelope that I open outside, on the street. One hundred and twenty dollars. I feel like I've won the one-hundred meter dash without taking any drugs.

Scene 12: The old guy who lived upstairs from me, back when I was on Saint-Hubert. Whenever we crossed paths on the stairway, he made me follow him into his room so I could look at his photo album full of smiling faces. But no one ever came to see him, and I lived in that building two years.

Springtime Song: The first day you can go out without a winter coat on. I go down Saint-Denis. The sun on my skin.

Behind the Frosted Window

On that December afternoon I was just
a shadow behind the frosted window
admiring
one of nature's most impressive spectacles.
Fascinated, I watched all that snow
endlessly falling.

The poet Émile Nelligan gained immortality
by using the word "snow" twice
in one very brief line:
"Oh, how the snow has snowed!"
Gilles Vigneault reached the same heights by singing
"My country is not a country, it's winter."
Here ice is the road to glory.

People of the North seem
so attracted by the sea
while ice frightens people of the South.
Is the seduction of hot weather enough
to explain why the first group
became colonizers much more easily
than the second?

No one saw it the way I did,
the snow falling
in fat gentle flakes.
I escaped the island
that seemed like a prison to me
and ended up encased
in a room in Montreal.

A short yellow dress slipping
through the cornfield
that dips down to the river.
I run behind my cousin.
The long summer vacation
still enchants my memory.

You can hear the song of the washerwomen
from the shack of that man
who lives off snail soup
and attends every funeral.

On my eyelids these images
burned by the sun of childhood.
Time moves at speeds so maddening
it has turned my life to a blur of colors.
That is how the polar night passes.

This sad gaiety always descends on me
at the same time.
When the car lights come on
and their beams sweep my room
and awaken my childhood terror.
I hide under the sheets.

The arrow makes
no noise in the night.
The pain visits
so suddenly
and will not depart
before dawn.

Night Train

In the train.
Time softens.
We let ourselves be lulled.
I awake with a start
when in the night we cross
a phantom train.

The livid faces
make me feel
this train is arriving from 1944.
A nightmare flash created
by fulguration (speed and light)
and my foggy brain.

We're in the middle of the countryside.
Pale glow lighting the houses.
I picture people gathered around the tv set.
The old man eating alone in his room.
The train won't slow down until we reach
the next city.

Brightly lit towers. Shadows stretching along the sidewalks.
And to think those robust trappers who once sold animal
hides to the Hudson's Bay Company have become elegant city-
dwellers drenched in perfume. The smell of eau de cologne
can't quite mask the stubborn scent of the forest—an autumnal
mixture of rain, green leaves and rotten wood. The vegetable
world isn't so far away. But yesterday's backwoodsmen have
become today's captives, glued to the small screen.

    I imagine it all happened gradually. A long series of conces-
sions led us to this new way of living. It's the same with
individuals. The crowd absorbs us one by one. Today, at age

fifty-six, I answer no to everything. I've needed more than half a century to recover the strength of character I had at the beginning. The strength of no. You have to keep at it. Stand behind your refusal. Hardly anything deserves a yes. Three or four things in a lifetime. Otherwise, answer no without hesitation.

The main thing in Protestant America is to make sure you never appear pretentious. Individually people want to slip through the cracks of life, but collectively they think they have a legitimate claim on the world. That kind of tension is not always bearable. Toward the end they can't stand it anymore and start spitting up all the bile they've kept hidden in the heart of their being. A flow of black blood. Too late they realize there were no rules. No paradise. They have sacrificed for nothing. A life wasted. And someone has to pay. Someone weaker they can wail away on with all their might. But just when they think they've found the energy to live, it's the end for them.

I escape into my thoughts
before sleep catches up to me.
The surrender is so sweet.
To fall asleep in one city
and wake up in another.

A Poet Named Césaire

The train pulls into the next station. The girl beside me who was reading a Tanizaki novel gets off. A young man waits for her with a bouquet of mimosas and furtive kisses. The platform empties. The couple is still fused, mouth to mouth now. The train pulls away. The girl forgot her book on the seat. She's already elsewhere. The book, like the train, served only to carry her to him.

I think back to my first suitcase forgotten in one of the city's narrow dusty rooms. Luckily I was able to hold onto the only things worth saving. A letter from my mother in which she explains, sparing no detail, how to live in a country she's never visited, and that dog-eared copy of *Notebook of a Return to the Native Land* by the Martinican poet Aimé Césaire. I still have both those things.

That phone call in the middle of the night. Are you Windsor Laferrière? Yes. This is the Brooklyn Hospital ... Windsor Laferrière has died. We have the same name.

They found my phone number in his pocket. The nurse who looked after him is on the line. In a soft, even voice she tells me he would come and see her when he wasn't feeling well. Sometimes his attacks were serious. No one else but me could get close to him at those times. A very sweet man despite the anger that was so strong inside him. Your father died smiling, that's all I can say. Lying on my back, I stare at the ceiling for a long while.

I get off in Toronto. A quick stop to see an old painter friend. We go for a drink in a bar near the gallery where he has a show. Since we're the same age the same things happened to us about the same time. His father died at the beginning of the year; he'd had to flee the country during the same period mine did. We're a generation of sons without fathers who were raised by women whose voices became even shriller when circumstances got too much for them. We end up drinking rum in his dark little studio. At dawn, he goes with me to the station.

I always travel with Césaire's collection of poems. I found it dull the first time I read it, nearly forty years ago. A friend had lent it to me. Today it seems strange that I could have read it at age fifteen. I didn't understand the devotion the book created among young people from the Antilles. I could tell it was the work of an intelligent man filled with terrible anger. I could feel his clenched jaw and imagine his eyes veiled in tears. I saw all those things, but not the poetry. The text seemed too prosaic. Too bare. Now, on this night, as I finally travel toward my father, suddenly I can feel Césaire's shadow behind his words. I can see how he went beyond his anger to discover new territories in his adventure with language. Césaire's striking images dance before my eyes. That all-powerful rage arises more from a desire to live in dignity than a will to denounce colonialism. The poet helps me draw the line between the pain that tears me apart and my father's subtle smile.

There is a photo of Césaire
sitting on a bench.
The sea behind him.
In a flowing khaki jacket
that makes him look like a frail bird.
His faded smile
and his wide eyes so gentle
do not reveal the rage
that changes him, before our eyes,
into a charred tree trunk.

Manhattan in the Rain

Umbrellas of every color. The air is so warm in New York
after the freezing weather in Montreal. My uncles are happy for
the warmth, though a bit surprised. It's almost like summer.
Manhattan in the tropics. My Uncle Zachée maintains that
nature is giving a gift to my father who hated the cold and
compared it to the injustice of men. The rain arrived too late
in his case.

A crowd in this big Manhattan church
for a man who lived alone
the last years of his life.
He was not forgotten.
Since he didn't want to see anyone,
people patiently awaited his death
to pay him tribute.

Now that he cannot flee
they burden him with compliments.
The sedentary like to see
the nomad made immobile.

Enclosed in a long box
he must think is a pirogue
that will let him skim across
the Guinaudée of his boyhood.

For many of these old Haitian taxi drivers, accompanied by
their wives, most of them nurses' aids at the Brooklyn Hospital
Center, he remained the young man who stood up to the power
and abuse of the President-for-Life. The glory of their youth.

It is the first time
I'm seeing him from so close.
I just have to reach out
my hand to touch him.
But I don't
to respect the distance
he wanted to maintain between us
during his life.

I remember that passage in the *Notebook* where Césaire demands
the body of Toussaint Louverture, arrested by Napoleon, killed
by the cold during the winter of 1803 in Fort de Joux, France.
His lips trembling with contained rage the poet comes to
demand, 150 years later, the frozen body of the hero of the slave
revolt: "What is mine a lone man imprisoned in whiteness."

A woman in a long white astrakhan coat
stands discreetly by the last column.
A ghost of a smile.
The smile of someone who knows
death can never erase
the memory of a certain summer afternoon
in an overheated room in Brooklyn.

Until the end,
even dirty,
even crazy,
my father remained
the dandy he'd always been.
Charm can't be explained.

I wonder who they're celebrating
when the one they're talking about
can't hear a word.
One of his old buddies is telling a story
that seems to amuse everyone.
I hear their laughter from a distance.

My father, very close by, in his casket.
I keep watch from the corner of one eye.
A star too blinding
to look at straight on.
That's what a dead father is.

One thing's for sure: my father won't have died until that
woman hears the news. And right now she is sitting on her
gallery in Port-au-Prince thinking, as usual, about him. Which
is what she has been doing every day since he left. Does she
know the wind has blown so hard these last days that it has
carried off the tree of which I am but a branch?

Outside it's a real tropical storm.
Broken tree branches.
Taxis drift, as if drunk,
down Fifth Avenue.
The hearse, unshakable, glides across the water.
It's like being in Baradères, my father's native village
and the Venice of Haiti, or so they say.

A Little Room in Brooklyn

My father lived in a little room that was practically empty.
My uncles took me there after the burial in the rain at the
Green-Wood Cemetery. Toward the end he had rid himself of
everything. All his life he was a solitary man though his political activities put him into contact with other people. Every day
for twenty years, summer and winter, he walked from Brooklyn
to Manhattan. His life could be summed up in that constant
movement. His only possession was the suitcase he had
entrusted to the Chase Manhattan Bank.

My father spent
more than half
his life
far from his land
from his language
and his wife.

Several years ago I knocked on his door. He didn't answer. I
knew he was inside the room. I could hear him breathing
noisily behind the door. Since I had come all the way from
Montreal, I insisted. I can still hear him yelling that he'd never
had a child, or a wife or a country. I had gotten there too late.
The pain of living far from his family had become so intolerable
he had to erase the past from his memory.

I wonder
when he knew
he would never
return to Haiti
and what exactly he felt
at that moment.

What did he think about
in his little room in Brooklyn
on those long frigid nights?
Outside was the spectacle
of the liveliest city in the world.
But in that room there was only him.
The man who had lost everything.
And so early in life.

I try to imagine him in his room, the blinds drawn, dreaming
of his city so similar to the one described by an angry young
Césaire: "And in this inert town, this squalling throng so
astonishingly detoured from its cry as this town has been from
its movement, from its meaning, not even worried, detoured
from its true cry, the only cry you would have wanted to hear
because you feel it alone belongs . . ." The cry is still stuck in the
poet's throat.

My uncles said I should meet his only friend in New York,
a barber on Church Avenue. He hadn't wanted to attend the
funeral. I always told Windsor I wouldn't go to his funeral. For
two good reasons. One: I don't believe in death. Two: I don't
believe in God . . . But that being said, I welcome with all due
honor the son of my last friend in this shitty life.

A customer wanted to assure him of his friendship. First,
you're not dead, and then you're not Windsor. He comes and
stands in front of me. You look a lot like him. I'm not talking
about physical resemblance, that's for fools who can't see any
farther than their noses. What I mean is that you were carved
from the same tree. Let me explain. Everyone laughs. Professor,
says my Uncle Zachée, we all understand what you mean. If you
say so . . . So then, young man, take a chair. And you can scram,
he says to another customer waiting to be looked after. I can

wait, I say, and go and sit near the washroom. Look, wasn't
I right to say they were carved from the same tree? There are
plenty of empty chairs and he goes and sits in the corner, in
Windsor's spot. He used to drink his coffee right there, every
morning for forty years. Only I could make it for him—me
and no one else. Not even my wife who loved him and did his
washing. Don't listen to people who tell you that Windsor
walked around in dirty clothes; that's not true. His wife,
standing next to the big portrait of Martin Luther King, agrees.
She went to the funeral because she still believes in God. As if
I'm not enough for her. Everybody laughs. Not him. Okay, now
it's your turn, Windsor. Windsor is dead and buried, Professor,
a customer says. That's my name too, I say. Why are they in
such a hurry to waste their breath? That's something I'll never
understand about these people. Only two men have the right
to express themselves at all times and they're both dead. One
was a prophet, and that's Martin Luther King. The other was a
madman, and that's Windsor. So shut up, the rest of you. I told
you Windsor isn't dead. You went to his funeral and the whole
time he's been sitting here quietly. In his spot. That's how I
inherited the chair near the washroom.

My uncles hold hands
as they walk to the bank.
Like children afraid
of losing their way in the forest.
That little act speaks for all their distress.
"Your father," Uncle Zachée speaks into my ear,
"walked straight ahead
as if he always knew where he was going."
Several people turn to look as we go by.

The Suitcase

We want to retrieve the suitcase my father deposited at the
Chase Manhattan Bank. Since I have the same first name, the
employee gives me the key to his safety deposit box and asks me
to follow him into the bank's vault. I step inside quietly with my
uncles. That quality of silence exists nowhere but in a bank, a
church or a library. Men fall silent only before Money, God and
Knowledge—the great wheel that crushes them. All around us,
small individual safety deposit boxes filled with the personal
belongings of New York, city of high finance and great misery.
The employee leaves us alone. I open my father's box and
discover an attaché case inside.

    I try to open it before realizing I need the secret code.
Numbers and letters. We try everything: his birth date and his
different given names, my birth date and my pseudonym. My
uncles give me all sorts of possible leads, even the date their
childhood friend met a violent death. As a last resort, we try his
last telephone number before his mind went adrift. Nothing
works. In the end, the employee returns, and we have to put the
suitcase back. I could not have taken it with me without first
answering a battery of questions that would have unmasked
me. I slip the suitcase back into the safety deposit box. The
employee closes the great vault of the Chase Manhattan Bank
behind us.

My uncles stand in disbelief
in front of the iron door.
I feel light
not having to carry such weight.
The suitcase of aborted dreams.

One of my uncles, the youngest,
suddenly takes me by the arm.
We almost slip on the wet pavement.
Your father was my favorite brother.
He was a very discreet man.
With each of us he maintained
a separate relationship.
Even if he always refused to live with us
he was very present in our lives.
In his own way, he concludes with a wink.

We choose a booth near the window in a restaurant that smells
very strongly of fried food, where my father would eat his
breakfast in Manhattan. The young waiter rushes over. Can we
still have breakfast? my Uncle Zachée asks. We serve breakfast
twenty-four hours a day here. And we always will as long as
someone in New York wants bacon and eggs and home fries.
My Uncle Zachée motions me over. He wants to introduce me
to the owner's wife who knew my father very well. She has very
white arms, a little mustache and that light in her eyes. Your
father ate lunch here every day. I wouldn't let him pay once
I knew his story. I couldn't have every exile eating here for
free—you can imagine how many there are in New York. But
his journey reminded me of my husband's. Both of them were
journalists and ambassadors before they got crossed off the list.
My husband was ambassador to Egypt and Denmark. At first
they talked about foreign policy the whole time. That was my
husband's passion. I bought this restaurant so he could meet
friends from his country and talk politics. Your father always
went to the cash before he left. He never took my generosity
for granted. I would refuse but he insisted. I handed him back

his money as if I were giving him his change. He stuffed it in
his pocket—not the type to count it. Did he even know what I'd
done? She laughs softly. I didn't do it out of pity. It was mostly
for my husband. I knew your father would never come back if he
thought he wouldn't be allowed to pay. So I arranged it so we'd
meet at the cash. And your husband? That's him by the window.
Sometimes he's okay, sometimes not. He's been expecting your
father all week. I can't bring myself to tell him he's dead.

I was four or five
when my father left Haiti.
He was in hiding more often than he was at home.
Here is the man at the origin of my life
and I don't even know how he tied his tie.

In the stifling loneliness of exile
one day he had the grand idea
of entrusting a suitcase to the bank.
I picture him strolling through the streets
after having put in a safe place
his most precious possession.

The suitcase was waiting for me.
He had faith in his son's reflex.
What he didn't know
(shut up, you can't teach a dead man anything)
is that destiny is not passed on from father to son.
That suitcase belongs to him alone.
The weight of his life.

Last Morning

I don't know why
this morning I have such a desire to see
my friend Rodney Saint-Éloi at 554 Bourgeoys Street.
Appreciate the irony of this street name
for a modest left-wing publishing house
in the working-class neighborhood of Pointe-Saint-Charles.

Waiting for me at the top of the steep staircase
Saint-Éloi and his wide smile
with a salmon cooking over low heat
on a bed of thin slices
of onion, tomato, lemon and red pepper.

Hanging on the wall the luminous poems
of Jacques Roumain, the young man who sang
so sadly of the fall of Madrid
with a feminine elegance
that reminds us of Lorca.

Here we are sitting,
Saint-Éloi and me.
Face to face.
Both of us from Haiti.
Him, scarcely five years ago.
Me, nearly thirty-five years back.
Thirty endless winters separate us.
That's the hard road he'll have to take.

He arrives just as
I'm leaving.
He's starting
as I finish.
Already the next generation.
So much time has passed.

One day, before him
will stand another man
who will resemble him
like a younger brother.
And he will feel
the way I do today.

The red sofa where this tall dark-haired girl is sleeping so
soundly. The night was eventful. Several empty wine bottles, a
make-up case, a black-and-yellow bra. The remains of a meal
still strewn across the table. Spices in small bottles. Towels on
the bathroom floor. Dirty dishes cluttering the sink. I step onto
the little balcony that overlooks the grassless yard. The life of
an intellectual in a working-class district.

  Tiga paintings on the walls. A photo of the poet Davertige
(light-colored suit, black bowler hat, big smile) in the vesti-
bule. His smile beneath the pain of a dandy at rest reminds me
of my father. Scattered here and there, the most recent books
published by Mémoire d'encrier: between the sheets, under the
bed, on the fridge, in the bathroom, even on the range where a
Creole-style chicken is simmering.

Exile combined with cold
and loneliness.
One year, in those conditions, counts as two.
My bones have dried out from inside.

Our eyes tired from seeing the same scene.
Our ears weary from hearing the same music.
We are disappointed at having become
what we have become.
And we understand nothing
of this strange transformation
that has occurred without our knowledge.

Exile in time is more pitiless
than exile in space.
I miss
my childhood more intensely
than my country.

I am surrounded by books.
I am falling asleep on my feet.
In my dream I see
my father's suitcase
tumbling through space.
And his judging eyes
turning slowly in my direction.

One last look out the airplane window.
This cold white city
where I've known my strongest passions.
Now ice lives inside me
almost as much as fire.

PART TWO

A Return

From the Hotel Balcony

From the hotel balcony
I watch Port-au-Prince
on the brink of exploding
by the turquoise sea.
In the distance, the island of Gonâve
like a lizard in the sun.

That bird that crosses
my field of vision
so quickly—barely eight seconds.
Here it comes again.
The same one?
As if that mattered.

The young man sweeping
the hotel courtyard so energetically,
so different from the old man yesterday morning,
seems to have his mind elsewhere.
Sweeping, because it lets you dream,
is a subversive activity.

This morning it's not Césaire
I feel like reading
but Lanza del Vasto
who was able to be satisfied
with a cool glass of water.
I need a man of serenity
not some guy seething with anger.

I don't want to think.
Just see, hear and feel.
Note it all down before I lose my head,
drunk on this explosion of tropical
colors, smells and tastes.
I haven't been part of a landscape like this
for so long.

In the slum called Jalousie (because of how close the luxury
villas are, which tells us something about the sense of humor
you need to live there) the little girl woke up before the others to
go fetch water. I follow her with the binoculars the hotel owner
lent me. She climbs the mountainside like a young goat, with a
plastic bucket on her head and another one in her right hand. I
lose sight of her as I scan the neighborhood waking up. There
she is again. Her wet dress flat against her thin young body. The
guy with the mustache and the tie sipping coffee on his gallery
watches her too.

Let us carefully observe the scene.
Close-up on the face of the mustached guy.
His intense concentration
on the dance of the girl's hips.
The slightest movement of that wonderfully supple body
is absorbed by his greedy little eyes.

The nose awakens to the scent.
The cat leaps.
Claws buried in the back of her neck.
The girl's arched back.
Not even a cry.
Everything happened
in his head
between two sips of coffee.

I sit on the veranda
and gently place the binoculars
at the foot of the chair.
Warmed by the sun
already strong at six in the morning
I soon slip into sleep
both light and deep.

Almost asphyxiated
by the smell of warm blood
that goes to my head.
The butcher is cutting
beneath my window.
The machete whistles.
A red rainbow in the air.
The cut throat of a young goat.

The animal seems to smile in its pain.
Its eyes, soft green, find mine.
What is there beyond such sweetness?
Its neck breaks
like a cane field bent low by the breeze.

Behind me the owner
smiles with her eyes.
Her long experience
of pain
should be taught
in these days
when we learn everything
except how to face
the storms of life.

The Human River

I step into the street
to bathe
in the human river
where more than one swimmer drowns
each day.

The crowd chews over the naïve fresh meat
of all those exiles who hope to recover
the years of absence in their energy.
I'm neither the first nor the last.

On the sidewalks.
In the parks.
In the middle of the street.
Everyone buying.
Everyone selling.
They try to trick poverty
through constant movement.

My eyes take in the scene.
Peasants listening to their transistors.
Hoodlums on motorbikes.
Girls working the street by the hotel.
The music of flies
above green mud.
Two bureaucrats slowly crossing the park.

Zoom in on that girl laughing on the sidewalk across the street
with a cell phone jammed in her ear. A car stops next to her.
Strident honking—as if the driver's hand were stuck on the
horn. The girl pretends not to hear. The driver goes on his way.
Laughter from the fruit vendors who witness the scene.

Primary colors.
Naïve motifs.
Childlike vibrations.
No space left empty.
Everything full to the brim.
The first tear will cause
this river of pain in which
people drown, laughing, to
overflow.

Proud carriage.
Empty belly.
The moral elegance of the girl
who walks past me
for the third time in five minutes.
Without a look in my direction.
Attentive to my slightest move.

Have you ever considered a city
of more than two million people
half of whom are literally starving to death?
Human flesh is meat too.
How long can a taboo
stand up to sheer necessity?

Fleshly desires.
Psychedelic visions.
Sidelong looks.
They'd like to devour
their neighbor for lunch.
Like one of those mangos
with such smooth skin.

A man whispers something into the ear
of his friend who smiles discreetly.
A gentle breeze lifts the woman's dress
as she runs laughing to hide behind a wall.
Drops so fine
I didn't realize it was raining.
Pain takes a time out.

This undecided lizard,
after much thought,
jumps from its branch.
A grass-green flash
cuts through space.

I am in this city
where nothing
for once
happens besides
the simple pleasure of being alive
under the blazing sun
at the corner of Vilatte and Grégoire Streets.

Hundreds of paintings covered in dust hang on the walls, all
along the street. They look as though the same artist painted
them all. Painting is as popular as soccer in this neighborhood.
The same luxuriant landscapes remind us that the artist doesn't
paint the real country but the country of his dreams.

I ask that barefoot painter
why he always paints trees bending low
under the weight of ripe heavy fruit
when everything around him is desolation.
You understand, he tells me with a sad smile,
who would want to hang in his living room
what he can see out the window?

What Happened to the Birds?

When I see that teenager sitting by himself
on the branch of a mango tree
strumming away on a battered old guitar,
I understand that amateur musicians
have taken over from the birds.
All that boy needs
is a pair of transparent wings.

A man who knew me thirty-five years ago comes up to me, arms
open. With abundant details and flying spittle, he conjures
up memories I'd completely forgotten and, worse, that don't
interest me. I try to avoid his eyes as we speak. What started as
a wonderful reunion has turned into torture. I'm waiting for
him to get to the point: money. In the end he moves on without
asking anything of me. I might have underestimated him. As I
walk, I try to retrace the thread of his story. Why didn't I listen
to him more carefully? Because of his dirty clothes, his black
fingernails, his toothless mouth? If he had been cleaner and
more prosperous, would I have paid him more attention? Even if
he opened the photo album of my teenage years before my eyes.

This old gentleman slightly bent at the waist
sweeping dry leaves
that have fallen into the courtyard of the city hall.
An activity that must take him all day.
From time to time, he sits down
but gets up with every breath of wind
that brings with it more dry leaves.

Not far away, on a yellow sofa that a little girl has just finished
cleaning, two businessmen are chatting as they wait to see the
mayor. People's voices cover the hushed tones of negotiation
between these men who have always lived in a world protected
by cash.

You have no idea
of the effect that new bills have
on people's eyes
in a country
where a worker makes
less than a dollar a day.

Last night, in front of the discotheque,
a teenage girl in a red miniskirt
and a tiny yellow blouse
screamed that she wasn't a whore
because "I don't want money,
I just want what you can buy
with money."

I am sitting under the hotel's almond tree
during the afternoon siesta.
A low pink wall
separates me from the street.
Life is on the other side.

Standing on the bench, I look over the wall at three young
women in front of a pyramid of brightly colored fruit. They
are talking among themselves so fast I can't make out what
they are saying. Their words interest me less than the beauty
of the scene.

What I see in the marketplace
is no different from what I see
in the little painting I just bought.
I look at the two scenes
unable to say
which one imitates the other.

A bird flies swiftly
into the clear hard noonday sky.
So thin but with an astonishing
determination to get as close
as possible to the sun.
It goes so far up
my eyes abandon the quest.

Death Doesn't Exist Here

A well-groomed young woman.
Black skirt below the knee.
She crosses the little square quickly
on her way to the phone booth
whose wire has been cut.
She sits down on a bench next to the phone.
Her head between her hands.

Men in black.
Women in tears.
Light rain despite the sun.
The little cemetery, hidden behind the marketplace,
is an oasis of peace.

Women in mourning though not widows
move among the dead
telling of their pain
without fear of being interrupted.
It's the only spot
where killers never come.

To live on a deforested island
knowing they'll never
see what is happening
on the other side of the water.
For most people
the hereafter is the only country
they have any hope of visiting.

A dog moves up the street.
Nose skyward.
Tail up.
It runs to the head
of the funeral procession.

I remember the pallbearers of my childhood
who danced with the casket on their shoulders.
Women threatening to throw themselves
into the hole to join their husband.
Frightened dogs running among the graves
while the wind shook the palm trees
like a schoolgirl playing with her braids
Death seemed so funny to me back then.

Later when I was a teenager
not a day would go by without
the bell tolling for someone.
Each time it made my mother's blood run cold.
Death that people compared to a journey
set my own mind wandering.

Death could come at any time.
A bullet in the back of the neck.
A red flash in the night.
It appeared so quickly we
never had time to see it coming.
Its speed made us doubt its existence.

Life in the Neighborhood (Before and After)

A quiet neighborhood.
Very discreet.
A vendor sets up her stall
near a wall.
Then a second one comes.
Then a third.
A week later
a new market has sprung up.
And life has changed in the neighborhood.

A man running with sweat
with a white plastic water pail.
He hides behind the low wall
and vigorously washes his face,
neck, torso and armpits.
Then returns to the market.

How can anyone think of other people when they haven't eaten
for two days and their son is at the General Hospital which
doesn't even have enough bandages? But that's exactly what that
woman did when she brought me a cool glass of water. Where
does she find such selflessness?

That's me in the yellowing photograph,
that thin young man from Port-au-Prince
in the terrible 1970s.
If you're not thin when you're twenty in Haiti,
it's because you're on the side of power.
Not just because of malnutrition.
More like the constant fear
that eats away at you from inside.

I remember the sun beating down on the backs of people's heads. Dusty street, no trees. We all had the same emaciated look (wild eyes and dry lips). That's how you could recognize our generation. We used to meet up in the afternoon in a little restaurant near Saint-Alexandre Square, with a view of the lumpy buttocks of anarchist poet Carl Brouard. This son of the solid bourgeoisie had chosen to wallow in the black mud, in the middle of the coal market, to share the poverty of the working-class people. There weren't just parlor poets tethered to corrupt power back then.

We discussed ad nauseam the absurdity
of this life while avoiding
references to the political situation
that were too obvious
because the poor quarters were crawling
with spies paid by the police.

Sharks in dark glasses
trawling the whorehouses patronized
by political science and chemistry
students who are always the first
to take to the streets.

I've been eating fat for three decades in Montreal
while everyone has gone on
eating lean in Port-au-Prince.
My metabolism has changed.
And I can't say I know what goes on
these days in the mind of a teenager
who doesn't remember
having eaten his fill
one single day.

My hotel is situated
in the center of a market.
At three o'clock in the morning
the vendors arrive.
The trucks full of vegetables are unloaded
and the racket runs nonstop
sometimes till eleven at night.

The power's out.
Impossible to read.
I can't sleep either.
Through the window, I watch the stars
that carry me back to childhood
when I would stay up late with my grandmother
on our gallery in Petit-Goâve.

I look at my poor body lying
on this hotel bed knowing
that my mind is wandering
down the passages of time.

I end up falling asleep.
Sleep so light
I can pick up the slightest sound.
Like those tourists
coming back from a night out.
There are so few tourists in this country
we should pay them to stay.

The high-pitched cry of a cat getting its throat cut.
At night alcoholics have a fondness
for that meat when it's grilled
with no concern for the panicked voice
calling everywhere for Mitzi.

Headache.
I can't sleep.
I go out on the veranda
and sit.

Something is moving up there.
A little girl
climbing the mountain
with a pail of water on her head.
Here we live on injustice and fresh water.

Drawing a Blank

The young man who sweeps
the hotel courtyard every morning
brings me a coffee and a message from my sister.
She didn't want to wake me
but my mother is not doing well.
She has locked herself in her room
and won't open the door for anyone.

Everyone looks pretty happy to me. My sister kisses me as she
dances. What's going on? Nothing. What about my mother?
That was this morning, now she's fine. It happens sometimes,
you know. In Montreal I would fall into an abyss without
warning and not surface for hours. The enemy, in Montreal,
is on the outside, when it's minus thirty for five days in a row.
Here the enemy is within, and the only nature we have to tame
is our own.

    I hear my mother singing. A song popular in her youth.
Radio Caraïbes often plays it on its oldies show, *Chansons
d'autrefois*. My sister whispers that she's often like this after one
of her descents into hell.

Marie, her name so simple
it's like
sharing my mother
with all my friends.

When I think about it I don't have any stories
about my mother from when she was young.
She's not the type to talk about herself.
Aunt Raymonde's stories are all
about her own person.
In vain I try to glimpse my mother
behind her.

My mother does not swim
in the great sea of History.
But all individual stories
are like rivers that run through her.
In the folds of her body she keeps
the crystals of pain of everyone
I have met in the street since I came here.

Pain.
Silence.
Absence.
None of that has anything to do
with folklore.
But they never
talk about those things
in the media.

Ghetto Uprising in the Bedroom

In my nephew's little room.
Books on a narrow shelf
next to a Tupac Shakur poster.
I spot one of my novels
and a collection of poems by his father.

My eyes seek out every detail
to help me travel back through the stream of time
and recover the young man
I was before my sudden departure.

We are sitting on the unmade bed
watching a documentary about violent gangs
battling each other in the lower reaches of the city.
Gunshots ring out.
From time to time, my mother comes in
and gives us a suspicious look.
My nephew is at the age when death
is still something esthetic.

From close range a Danish television crew is following
the violent confrontations that have been raging
for months in this miserable district.
Graffiti on a wall shows an empty stomach
and a toothless mouth holding a gun
heavier than the weight of the average adult
in that part of town.

A young French woman
has entered this seething slum.
Close-ups on the two brothers as sensitive
as cobras in the sun.
Each heads his own gang.

The young woman travels back and forth
between the two brothers.
One loves her.
She loves the other.
A Greek tragedy in Cité Soleil.

Bily is obsessed by his younger brother
who took on the name Tupac Skakur.
Fascination with American culture
even in the poorest regions
of the fourth world.

I watch the two brothers
strolling through the Cité.
Undernourished killers.
Emaciated faces.
Cocaine to burn.
Weapons everywhere.
Death never far.

I wonder what my nephew
thinks about all this.
It's his culture.
The new generation.
Mine was the '70s.
We're all cloistered in our decades.

These days the murderer strikes at noon
in this country.
Night is no longer the accomplice of the killer
who dreams of adding his star to the firmament.
To reach the heavens nowadays
they have to kill with their face uncovered
and trumpet their acts on the tv news.

The Tonton Macoutes of my era had
to hide behind dark glasses.
Serial killers.
Papa Doc was the only star.

Tupac, the young leader who looks so much like Hector,
has conquered the Foreign Woman.
Tonight their savage kiss
on a reed mat on the floor
will drive all the warriors crazy
under the Cité ramparts.

Now Tupac is making political speeches.
He moves through Cité Soleil in a car.
Thinking he's a real leader.
A loud voice and an itchy trigger finger.
Suddenly he becomes lucid and
sees himself for what he is: a loser.

Facing the camera.
Sitting in the shadows.
Tupac: "If I stop, I'm a dead man.
If I go on, I'm a dead man."
I feel my nephew shiver as if
he were facing the same choice.

This is a city where the killers
all want to die young.
Tupac falls at the height of his glory
in the dust of Cité Soleil.
Like his brother Bily.
Both killed by a frail young man
who suddenly stepped from the shadows.

The girl leaves with the tv crew.
On the cassette there's blood, sex and tears.
Everything the viewer wants.
Roll the credits.

An Emerging Writer

My nephew wants to be a famous writer.
The influence of the rock-star culture.
His father is a poet who gets death threats.
His uncle, a novelist living in exile.
He has to choose between death and exile.
For his grandfather it was death in exile.

Before you begin
you have time to think about fame
because once you write the first sentence
you're up against
this anonymous archer
whose real target is your ego.

Later on.
In a comfortable armchair.
By the fireside.
Fame will come.
Too late.
The hope then will be
for a day without suffering.

The worst stupidity, it seems,
is to compare one era
to the next.
One man's time
to another's.
Individual times
are parallel lines
that never touch.

In the little room, my nephew and I
look without seeing each other.
We try to understand
who the other is.
On the narrow shelf I notice
some Carter Brown novels that once belonged to me.

To write a novel, I tell my nephew
with a sly smile,
what you really need is a good pair of buttocks
because it's a job
like the seamstress's
where you spend a lot of time sitting down.

You also need a cook's talents.
Take a large kettle of boiling water,
add some vegetables
and a raw piece of meat.
You'll put in the salt and spices later
before lowering the heat.
All the flavors will blend into one.
The reader can sit down to the feast.

It's like a woman's job,
my nephew points out, worried.
It's true you have to be able to change
into a woman, a plant or a stone.
All three realms are necessary.

Watching the vein in his temple beat that way, I know he's
thinking fast. But you haven't explained the most important
thing to me. What would that be? It's not just the story, it's how
you tell it. Then what? You have to tell me how to do it. You don't

want to write something personal? Of course. No one can tell you how to be original. There must be tricks that can help. It's always better if you discover them yourself. But I'll waste time. That's the point: time doesn't exist in this job. I feel like I'm all alone. And lost. What good is having an uncle who's a writer if he tells you he can't help you out? At least you know that much. A lot of young writers think they can't write because they aren't part of a network. Maybe I don't know how to write. You can't say that if you haven't spent at least a dozen years trying to find out. What do you mean? A dozen years to find out I can't write? Well, believe me, that's a conservative figure. So what good is the experience then? I can't tell you any more than that, Dany.

My sister's son is called Dany.
We didn't know you were going to come back, my sister told me.
The exile loses his spot.

He goes and gets himself a glass of juice, then he's back on the subject. One last question: is it better to write by hand or on a computer? It's always better to read. Okay, I can see I'm not going to get anything out of you, he says, then takes a Carter Brown novel from the shelf and heads for the bathroom.

On the little gallery.
I am sitting.
He is standing.
A respectful distance.
You never talk about your times.
I don't have a time.
We all do.
I'm sitting here with you, that's my time.
The cry of a bird that can't stand
the noonday heat.

My aunt takes me aside,
in a dim room
where the furniture is covered with white sheets,
and rattles on and on about some
endless family saga
whose protagonists
are unknown to me and whose claims
are so confusing
that even she gets lost.
It's like being in a novel
by a sloppy writer.

My nephew goes to meet a friend
by the gate.
I watch them talking.
Their affection
for each other.
They share the same tough choice:
stay or go.

City of Talk

This man sitting alone,
his back against the gate,
is soon joined by a stranger
who begins telling him all sorts of things
that make absolutely no sense.

Hunting down the solitary man
is a collective passion
in any overcrowded city.

A tank truck parked
on the sidewalk across the way.
I watch my mother
favoring one leg
cross the street to
buy bottled water.
I never knew crossing a street
required so much willpower.

Christian, a nine-year-old neighbor
who spends a lot of time at our house,
comes and sits next to me.
We go almost an hour without talking.
A good breeze blows through the leaves.
I soon drift off.
The boy slipped away so quietly
I thought I'd dreamed him up.

My nephew tells me
he burned his first novel.
All good writers start by
being pitiless critics.
Now he has to learn
a little compassion for his work.

My nephew and I sit together on his squeaky narrow bed. I read detective novels, that's how I relax after a day at the university. A lot of hard work? Actually, we don't do anything at all. What do you do? Everyone is waiting for their American visa, and once they get it, even if it's in the middle of an exam, they take off.

A leaf, near me,
falls.
No sound.
What elegance!

A dull thud.
The noise a fat lizard makes
as it falls by my chair.
We consider each other a moment.
In the end it gets interested
in a spinning fly.

I listen to the radio.
A silky voice like a veil
that obscures the truth without managing to hide it.
People always have some story to tell
in a country where words are
the only thing they can share.

The music dies suddenly.
No sound.
Emptiness.
A power failure?
Endless silence in the street.
Then a cry of pain from the young girl next door.

To be able to hear silence this loud
in a city of talk
means so many people had to
keep quiet at the same time.

The radio announces
the death of a young musician
beloved by the public.
My nephew knew him well
having shared with him
for a brief moment
a girl's heart.

My nephew changes clothes quickly. My mother's worried look.
The banged-up Chevrolet parks on the sidewalk across the way.
Five of them are inside. Two girls in back. My nephew slips in
between them. His face immediately transformed. The car pulls
away. On the radio is the singer who just died. My sister looks
straight ahead without a word. Now I see what my mother's
face looked like when I went out like that on a Saturday night.
We would cross paths near Saint-Alexandre Square, on Sunday
morning, as she was going to church and I was coming back
from a party.

My Mother's Song

We are on the gallery.
By the oleander.
My mother is speaking to me softly of Jesus,
the man who replaced her husband
in exile for the last fifty years.
In the distance the voice of a woman selling baubles.

Every family has its absent member in the group portrait. Papa
Doc introduced exile to the middle class. Before, such a fate was
reserved only for a president who fell victim to a coup or one of
those rare intellectuals who could also be a man of action.

I took all possible precautions
before announcing to my mother
that my father had died.
First she turned a deaf ear to me.
Then took it out on the messenger.
The distance is so slight
between lengthy absence and death
that I didn't take enough care
to consider the effect the news would have on her.

My mother won't look at me.
I watch her long delicate hands.
She slides her wedding band
on and off her finger
and hums so softly
I have trouble understanding the words of her song.

Her gaze is lost in the clump of oleander
that reminds her of a time
when I did not yet exist.
The time before.
Is she recalling those days when she was
a carefree young woman?
Her fleeting smile moves me more than tears.

I hear my mother singing
from the room next door.
The news of my father's death
has finally reached her consciousness.
Sorrow is her daily escort,
the empty days
alternating with the magic of the first smile.
Everything resurfaces.

I finally catch a few words
of my mother's song
that speaks of panicked sailors,
rough seas
and a miracle just when
all hope seems lost.

She likes to listen to the radio on the little set I sent her a few
years back. Tuned to the same prayer station. She listens only to
sermons and religious music except for *Chansons d'autrefois*, the
show where the singers hit notes so high they make the old dog
whimper from under the chair where it sleeps.

I go back and forth from the hotel
to the house hidden behind the oleander.
My mother is surprised I won't stay
with her.

It's because I don't want to give her the illusion
we're living together again
when my life has gone on without her
for so long.

I keep coming back to her
in everything I write.
I spend my life interpreting
the slightest shadow on her brow.
Even from a distance.

Her Sadness Dances

As I get dressed I think of that woman
who spent her life taking care of other people.
It's a way of hiding too.
Now for the first time she is laid bare.
My mother in her naked pain.

I'm in a friend's car on the way to her house. I remember
we never listened to music back then. The radio was just for
the news. All it played were the same speeches celebrating
the glory of the President. They went so far we sometimes
wondered whether he didn't smile at all that flattery. He was
compared to the greatest men, even to Jesus once. My mother
reacted with a burst of dry laughter. We had to pretend we
were listening so the neighbors wouldn't suspect us of not
supporting the regime. We turned up the volume. Our neighbors did the same. An atmosphere of collective paranoia.
Those were dark years. Our blood ran cold every time we heard
classical music. Right after, they would announce a failed
coup, which was always a pretext for carnage. I ended up asso-
ciating classical music with violent death.

Every morning, on the radio, a stentorian voice
would remind us of our oath to the flag
followed by the nasal voice of Duvalier
himself who would declare "I am the flag, one and
indivisible." I've been allergic to political speeches
ever since.

I picture my mother dancing
with a chair
in the shadows of the little living room.
She dances her sadness at five o'clock
in the afternoon.
Like a Lorca poem
about Franco's bloody nights.

My mother loved numbers. Every morning she made her budget
of the day's expenses in a school notebook. Since she was
always short of money, having lost her job right after my father
left, she spent hours counting and recounting the few coins
she had. Endless calculations. I do the same thing today, but
with words. The bank was farther from my mother than the
dictionary is from my hand.

The neighbor boy lets me know with a nod of his head
that my mother has fallen asleep again
still humming her song about the sailors
lost at sea to whom an angel appeared.
I use the break to talk with my sister
in the room at the back
where it's as hot as an oven.

My sister is even more secretive than my mother.
Seeing her constant smile it's hard to imagine
she lives in a country ravaged by dictatorship
like a hurricane
that has been punishing the island for twenty years.

She tells me about her life at work where people call her a snob because she makes a point of buying a novel as soon as she gets paid and because she wears perfume to the office. The more she treats people with respect, the more they plot against her. As if she reminded them of that precious thing they have lost along the way: their own self-respect.

My sister talks calmly
without looking at me.
She is like a little girl forgotten
by her parents in the dark woods
who wonders how long it will take
before the pack catches up to her.

Back at the house, she discovers her mother sitting on the gallery, silent and sad. My mother who was once so light-hearted. Of course I look after her expenses, but my sister has to face the travails of daily life. She's forced to watch my mother's health deteriorate, and struggle through her dark days: "I'm afraid one day I'll be too worn out to go get her at the bottom of the well." This time she looks at me, and I see the years of my absence written on her face. We remain silent for a time. Then slowly a smile blooms. The dark cloud has passed.

Sitting in the darkened living room with my sister, I watch my mother go about her evening business. She inspects the kitchen down to the last crumb before lighting the lamp and placing it in the middle of the table. Then she scrapes the remains of the meal into a blue plastic bowl. Only then does she sit down to eat. That's her ritual.

Why is she eating from this plastic bowl when I sent her a new set of dishes? From underneath the sofa my sister pulls out the big box of silverware that has never been removed from its packaging. She doesn't like it? On the contrary—it's her treasure. She takes it out once a month and cleans it. In the lamplight, her face is serene. She is still beautiful. She is wearing her face for special days. As soon as you leave, my sister tells me, she'll put her dark-day face back on.

I am overcome with such a feeling of remorse.
The feeling that everything is wasted.
My mother, and then my sister.
The women have paid the price in this house.

I go out to see my nephew on the gallery. He was listening to the news on my mother's transistor radio. I sit next to him. Do you ever dream? Yes, but I don't remember. I used to dream every night when I was young, and every morning I would tell my grandmother my dream. Why? At the time, we would tell our dreams. Anyway, I always dreamed the same dream. Actually, I had two kinds of dreams. In the first, I had wings. I flew over the town. And I slipped through the window of certain houses to watch girls I was in love with sleep. My nephew laughs. And the second kind? I dreamed of the devil. The same thing every time. All of a sudden we heard a terrible racket. The devils were coming. We hurried to get inside before they showed up. You never knew that house, I say to my nephew. My mother talks about it all the time. It was a big house with lots of doors and windows. It feels like a century ago... We tried to close them. But the devils were everywhere. When we closed a door, they came in through the window. Nowadays, those devils have been replaced by real killers in the light of day. But I keep having the same dreams wherever I go. In hotel rooms all around the world. That's the only thing that hasn't changed with me. I have the same ritual: I lie down between white sheets, read a while, then turn off the light and drop into a universe full of devils. You should keep holy water in your suitcase. That's what my grandmother used when I had nightmares. But I treasure those dreams. They're the only thing that's left of my life from before.

My mother and my sister
come out to be with us
on the gallery.
A choir singing religious music on the radio.
My mother accompanies them.
Evening falls.

A Social Problem

A cold face in the pale early morning light.
A young shark in a Cardin shirt
striding swiftly to his car
seems as insensitive to life as to death.

To survive if only morally
in this city where the rules change
according to the customer's looks,
the rich man has to avoid
meeting the poor man's eyes.

Every hour
the exchange rate for the gourde changes.
Even if money is concentrated
in the same hands.
What can such financial frenzy mean
on an island abandoned by the birds?

He rushes from his house to his car,
from his car to his office,
from his office to the restaurant
and from the restaurant to his seaside house
where he'll meet his mistress of the month.
He may know nothing of the poor man
but the poor man is watching his every move.
The rich man is a creature of habit.

What good is being rich in a country
constantly at the mercy of a bread riot?
The chances of losing a fortune
overnight are high.
A can of gas and the whole neighborhood goes up.
The game changes so fast.
One starving guy with a match
calls the shots.

Why stay in this mudhole mixed with shit trampled by crowds hemmed in by malarial anopheles when you could lead a dream life somewhere else? Here the rich man must collect the poor man's money. And he can't delegate an operation like that, considering the country's current moral state. People have no scruples about keeping money for themselves that they figure is stolen. The debate raging these days in the poor districts where Christian morality has gotten its hooks in can be summarized by this mighty question: is it theft to steal from a thief? The State says yes. The Church does too. But what if just once the question wasn't put to them? The pressure is strong on the ill-paid office clerk who has to deliver to the boss, down to the last penny, all the money gathered in the poorest districts of the hemisphere. All those houses with neither roof nor door rented to large needy families by usurers representing the rich who live in the luxury villas set high up the mountain. We're really living in Victor Hugo's *Les Misérables*.

When I went North, I had to rid myself
of the heavy reality of the South
that oozed from every pore.
I spent thirty-three years adapting
to that winter country where everything is so different
from what I'd known before.

Returning South after all these years
I am like someone
who has to relearn what he already knows
but had to forget along the way.

I admit that it's easier
to learn than to relearn.
But harder still
is to unlearn.

The Blind Archer

Noise was the path the Caribbean used
to enter me.
I had forgotten the racket.
The bellowing crowd.
The overabundance of energy.
A city of beggars and rich men
awake before dawn.

You can find the same energy
in a naïve painting
where the vanishing point
is not at the back of the canvas
but in the solar plexus
of the viewer.

When you look at a market scene
by any street painter
you don't feel you're entering
the marketplace but that
instead the market
is entering you, overwhelming you
with smells and tastes.
Which is why you step back
faced with these strong primary colors.

People die faster here than elsewhere,
but life is more intense.
Each person carries the same amount
of energy to burn
except the flame is brighter
when the time it has to burn
is briefer.

Behind me, the blue mountains
that surround the city.
This dawn sky with its rosy hue.
A man is still sleeping
under a truck packed with melons.

In the international media
Haiti always appears deforested.
Yet I see trees everywhere.
As a child I hated trees
so much I dreamed of covering the planet in asphalt.
People always wanted to know why
a child wouldn't like trees.
It was that feeling they were looking down on me.

Two hearses cross paths
on this dusty street
at the foot of the mountain.
Each one is carrying its customer
to his resting place.
The last taxi costs the most.

Death, that blind archer.
As busy at midnight as at noon.
Too many people in this city
for him, even once,
to miss his target.

All I need is to start the rumor
that I've returned to live there
without saying which *there* it is
and in Montreal people will believe
I'm in Port-au-Prince
and in Port-au-Prince they'll be sure
I'm still in Montreal
Death would mean not being
in either of those cities.

To Die in a Naïve Painting

I like to climb up the mountain, early in the morning, to get a closer look at the luxury villas set so far apart one from the other. Not a soul around. Not a sound, except the wind in the leaves. In a city this populous, the space you have to live in defines who you are. In my random walks, I discover that these vast properties are inhabited only by servants. The owners reside in New York, Berlin, Paris, Milan or even Tokyo. Like in the days of slavery when the real masters of Hispaniola lived in Bordeaux, Nantes, La Rochelle or Paris.

They built these houses hoping their children studying abroad would return to take the family business in hand. Since those children refuse to return to a country cast into darkness, the parents have moved closer to them and settled in some metropolis with a museum, a restaurant, a bookstore or a theater on every corner. The money harvested from the mud of Port-au-Prince is spent at Bocuse or La Scala. In the end the villas are rented out for a fortune to the directors of non-profit international aid organizations whose stated goal is to lift the country out of poverty and overpopulation.

These envoys from humanitarian organizations show up in Port-au-Prince with the best intentions. Lay missionaries who look you straight in the eye as they recite their program of Christian charity. In the media they are prolix about the changes they intend to create to ease the terrible conditions of the poor. They make a quick tour of the slums and the ministries to take the pulse of the situation. They learn the rules of the game so quickly (allow themselves to be served by a host of servants and slip part of the budget allocated to the project into their pockets) you have to wonder whether it's in their blood—an atavism of colonial times. When confronted with their original project, they escape by saying that Haiti is incapable of change. Yet in the international press, they go on denouncing corruption in the country. The journalists passing through know they have to stop in for a drink poolside to gather the solid information they need from honest and objective people; the Haitians, everyone knows, can't be trusted. The journalists never ask themselves why these people are living in villas when they say they've come to help the wretched of the earth throw off the shackles of poverty.

Haiti has undergone thirty-two coups
in its history
because people have tried to change
things at least thirty-two times.
The world is more interested by the military men
who engineer the coups
than by the citizens who overthrow
those men in uniform.
Silent, invisible resistance.

There is a balance in this country
based on the fact
that unknown people
in the shadows
are doing everything they can
to put off the arrival of night.

When there's a power failure,
people light their houses
with the energy of sexually charged bodies.
The only fuel this country has
in industrial quantities
can also send
the demographic curve soaring.

When you arrive in this city set on the shores of a turquoise sea and surrounded by blue mountains, you wonder how long it will take before it all becomes a nightmare. In the meantime you live with the energy of someone waiting for the end of the world. So said a young German engineer who's been working for the last ten years rebuilding the road network.

We were having a drink at the bar at the Hotel Montana. When did you first understand that this particular hell wasn't for you? He gazed at me a while. My father came here for the New Year's holiday, and he made me see it. My father is an old military man. His job is to look at things as they are and say what he thinks in no uncertain terms. What did he say to you? That we were all bastards in this well-protected luxury hotel, all the while thinking we were living a dangerous and difficult life. And so? And so ten years later I'm still here. But at least I'm not telling myself any more lies. We can even use cynicism to keep from dying of shame.

The headquarters of foreign journalists.
A hotel set on the heights so they can see
what's boiling over down below
in the great stewpot of Port-au-Prince
without actually having to go there.
For the details just listen to the local radio station.
The bar is stocked well enough to resist a month-long siege.

I've been watching this cameraman at the end of the bar for a while. His arm resting lightly on his camera. I move down to his end because I like people whose job is to look. But I don't see anything, he tells me. I see only what I'm filming. I look down a very narrow field. People are incredible here. They participate in everything, they're so enthusiastic. I've been to a lot of countries with the job I do, but this is the first time I've seen anything like it. You can ask someone whose family has just been killed to reenact the scene, and they'll play the whole thing for you with complete attention to detail. The murderer too: just ask him and he'll play the murderer for you. It's a real pleasure working here. Wherever I go people ask for money, but not here. Okay, friends of mine told me the market ladies want to be paid if you take their picture, but that's only if they don't like you. That's because some photographers don't know how to go about it. They want to go too fast. Here, you can't hurry people. They have their dignity. They can feel it right away if you respect them, and if they feel you're making fun of them then I can tell you your life is in danger. Otherwise, they're cool. And the setting is magnificent, not too green so it doesn't look like a postcard, it's great, I really can't complain. Excuse me, it's your country and I'm talking this way, I'm not insensitive to what's happening, I see the poverty and everything, but I'm speaking as a professional. All jobs are like that; if you could hear the surgeons when they operate on you, they opened me up three times, and it's curious but hearing them talk about what they had for dinner the night before as they were slicing me up, that reassured me because I knew they were doing it to relax. I'm not insinuating that people are insensitive to their own misfortune, it's just that they like to play, to act, they're born comedians, and what does a comedian do when the camera goes on? He acts. The kids, especially the kids—they're so natural. And in a setting like this. It's like nothing is real here. I listen to the big shots talking, I cover the press conferences at the palace, receptions at the embassies, and I can tell you, if you don't mind, that the only thing that will get this country out of the state it's in is the movies. If the Americans forgot about Los Angeles and came and shot their blockbusters here and if the Haitian government was smart enough to demand a quota, yes, I said a quota of Haitian actors on every film, in less than twenty years you'd see this country get out of this mess, and the money would be clean money too because these people are fabulous actors. And the sets too, they're so colorful, very, very alive. I never thought you could die in a landscape like this.

Hunger

I woke up
in the middle of the night.
My nerves jangling.
My pajamas completely soaked.
As if I had swum
through a sea of noise.

From that tiny house,
just three rooms
protected only by walls as thin
as fine paper,
I saw no fewer than thirty-six people
come out
in less than an hour.
Not a millimeter left unoccupied.
Not a second of silence, I imagine.

We search for life
among the poor
in absolute uproar.
The rich have bought up the silence.

Noise is concentrated
in a clearly defined perimeter.
Here trees are scarce.
The sun, implacable.
Hunger, constant.

In this space teeming with people.
First comes the obsession with the belly.
Empty or full?
Sex comes right after.
And after that, sleep.

When a man prefers
a plate of beans and rice
to the charming company of a woman
something has happened
to the hierarchy of taste.

The pattern has become common. The rich who flee the poor
leave the city behind and go to live in ever more secluded
parts of the countryside. It's not long before the news spreads
through the overpopulated zone. The siege begins. A little hut
in a ravine. Another at the foot of the pink villa. Two years later
a whole slum has sprung up, asphyxiating the new upper-class
quarter. The goal of all wars is the occupation of territory.

    The space of words can be occupied as well. For the last hour,
this toothless old woman has been telling me a story of which
I understand nothing. Yet I feel that it's hers and it is worth, in
her eyes, as much as anyone else's.

A day here lasts a lifetime.
You're born at dawn.
You grow up at noon.
You die at twilight.
Tomorrow you change bodies.

The horn has a variety of uses. Sometimes it replaces the cock's
crow. It alerts the absent-minded pedestrian. It announces a
departure or an arrival. It expresses joy or anger. It carries on
an endless monologue in traffic. To outlaw the horn in Port-au-
Prince would be censorship.

    I walked into an Internet café and discovered a friend I
hadn't seen for some time. My old comrade Gary Victor with
his moon-like face always makes me think of sweet-tempered

Jasmin Joseph, the man who painted nothing but rabbits. Every time, Gary Victor pulls out of his hat a novel full of devils, thieves, zombies, mocking spirits and carnival bands painted in the cheerful colors of a naïve painting. But so loaded down with obsessions that in the end it becomes as dark as a teenage nightmare. I talked with him for a while about what the subject of the great Haitian novel might be. First we reviewed the obsessions of other nations. For North Americans, we thought it was space (the West, the Moon landing, Route 66). For South Americans, it's time (*One Hundred Years of Solitude*). For Europeans, it's war (two world wars in a century alters the mind). For us, it's hunger. The problem, Victor told me, is that it's difficult to talk about it if you haven't known it. And those who've seen it up close aren't necessarily writers. We're not talking about being hungry just because you haven't eaten for a while. We're talking about someone who has never eaten his fill in his entire life, or just enough to survive and be obsessed by it.

Still, it's very surprising how hunger is absent, considering that artists are always looking for subjects. Very few novels, plays, operas or ballets have hunger as their central theme. Yet there are a billion starving people in the world today. Is the subject too harsh? We don't mind exploiting war, epidemics and death in every possible shape. Is the subject too raw? Sex is stretched across every screen on the planet. So what's going on? The problem is that hunger concerns only people who have no buying power. Starving people don't read, don't go to museums, don't dance. They just wait to die.

Food is the most terrifying of drugs. We always go back to it: three times a day for some, once in a while for others. Gary Victor told me he never knew the great famine. Me neither. Which made us think we'd never be the authors of the great

Haitian novel whose subject can only be hunger. Roumain touched upon it by making drought the subject of *Masters of the Dew*. Drought is thirst. The earth that is thirsty. I'm talking about a man who is hungry. Of course the earth feeds man. I tried to console Victor by bringing up subjects that could be as interesting, like exile, but that theme doesn't stand up to a man who is hungry. When we parted, he had a certain sadness in his eyes.

But it's not just the subject of a novel.
We can be impassive
faced with our own hunger but what do we do
when a child is hungry
and reaches out his hand
as happened this morning near the market?
We give him a few pennies
knowing full well the problem
will return in less than three hours.

This man sitting in the shade
by the wall of the hotel.
On a handkerchief he sets
a large purple avocado next to a long loaf of bread.
He slowly produces his jackknife.
This is his first meal of the day.
Such pleasure is unthinkable
for those for whom eating
is not the primary goal of existence.

At ninety-eight this lively, joyful old lady
who runs the Hotel Ifé
and who still fights every day
to keep her head above water
with a smile that never fades
is the mother of a poet friend.

In this country the poet's mother
has to work till her dying day
so that roses can flower
in her son's verses.
He preferred to go to prison
than to work.

Here we are wedged into a corner of a little restaurant in my
old neighborhood. A simple meal: rice, avocado, chicken. I like
restaurants that serve just one dish. You get there, you sit down
and you talk until the food arrives. I was eating, head down,
when I spotted a beggar watching me from behind the window
with wide liquid eyes so much like my mother's.

My Nephew's Version

My nephew is doing the talking tonight.
Back against the wall.
Calm and resolved.
We listen to what he has to say.
He is telling today's life story.

How does he see things?
What does he feel?
We want to know.
He knows that too and embellishes.
Once I was in his position.

Standing by the door,
my mother smiles.
She has listened to three generations of men,
if we count my father,
each telling
a new version
of the same facts.

My grandmother Da. My mother Marie. My sister Ketty. These
women don't concern themselves with History but with daily
life, which is an endless ribbon. No time to look back when
every day means serving three meals to the children, rent to pay,
shoes to replace, medicines to buy, money for Friday afternoon
soccer, Saturday night movies and the Sunday morning church
fair. Just because you're crushed by dictatorship doesn't mean
you have to live poorly.

The most subversive thing there is,
and I've spent my life repeating it,
is to do everything possible to be happy
under the dictator's nose.

The dictator insists on being the center of your life
and what I did best in mine
was to banish him from my existence.
I admit, to do that sometimes I had to throw
the baby out with the bathwater.

So I left and then returned. Things haven't changed a bit. Going
to see my mother this evening, I crossed the market. The lit
lamps made me feel I was traveling through a dream. A little
girl in a short pink jersey dress was sleeping in the arms of her
mother who was counting the day's receipts. This tenderness
that lets you accept the rest exhausted me and will soon exhaust
my nephew.

The people in this neighborhood,
in these modest houses on both sides of the ravine,
earn a salary
on which
it is impossible to live.
By "live" you must understand:
the simple ability to feed oneself.

The other features of life,
like going to the movies
or buying an ice cream
on a Sunday afternoon,
have grown so distant
they no longer concern them.
If they are mentioned it's only out of nostalgia.

When a few Dior-soaked gentlemen
mix every day
with a dense crowd stinking of piss:
the war of the smells.

I know the solution
is not to go for your neighbor's jugular.
At least that's what's said
in certain parlors.
But just how long
can this kind of tension last?

My nephew doesn't put it that way
but in his head I can hear
a familiar wave of background noise.
He doesn't want to worry my mother
whose husband and only son had to go into exile
for the same reasons.
It's up to the third generation
to ask the question that has no solution.

A leaf falls from the tree
onto the notebook where
I am writing these things down.
I save the leaf.
I can't keep my eyes off
that black bird
with the long yellow beak.

I don't see things the way I used to, my nephew tells me. How
did you used to see them? I ask without trying to figure out
what things he's talking about. Like things that are happening
in my life. And now? Like things that are happening around
me. What do you mean? I feel more distance between me and
reality. Maybe that's your space for writing.

The Dead Are among Us

My nephew drives me back to the hotel. We are in his friend
Chico's car, and we have to keep our feet directly below our
legs because there's no floor. We can see the asphalt go by
and puddles of greenish water. The car is like a convertible in
reverse. His brother left him the car when he went to Miami,
and four of them use it. Put some gas in it and it's yours. When
it breaks down, they chip in and take it to a mechanic. Chico is
set to go next week and he'll leave the car to his friends. They
take turns using it but they all have to go to the same club on
Saturday night. With their girlfriends that makes eight. A pretty
tight squeeze. The girls insist on paying the Saturday night gas.

I turn around to see
my mother standing near the big red gate.
She must have woken up suddenly and gotten dressed
in a hurry when she understood I was leaving.
That tense face I know so well.
As if she sensed constant danger.

The last image of my mother
as the car goes around the curve:
I see her take the hand of the little boy next door,
her last confidant.

My nephew drops me off near the square.
I feel like watching the evening
settle over Pétionville.
Those who haven't wandered through a city
at night don't really know it.

I sit down across from city hall
to listen to Wagner's tetralogy
that the mayor has played every evening.

A man sits down quite close to me.
He talks to me through half-closed eyes,
his hands hang between his legs.
His conversation is punctuated
by long conspiratorial silences.
It takes him half an hour
to realize we don't know each other.
He puts his hat back on before disappearing
into the shadows.

My mother told me this afternoon
in the voice of someone
who knows she's being listened to
that the dead walk among us.
You can recognize them by the way
they appear and disappear
without us knowing why they were there.

Lost Things and Lost People

The worker's day is so well regulated he no longer feels the day's heat. We can understand why the first thing the silk workers did in their rebellion was to shoot at the cathedral clock. They recognized their ancestral enemy. Every second is a drop of blood.

I can't really make out objects.
The sleep that comes to me
between two explosions of noise
is like an uppercut.
This isn't sleep.
This is a knockout.

I've been awake for a while, and I feel like I've been put through the mill. My body is suffering an adaptation process that's beyond my will. I am the master of nothing. Everything I banished from my mind back there in order to live without the bonds of nostalgia has a concrete presence here. Those things sought refuge in my body where the cold froze them in place. Now my body is slowly warming. My memory is thawing: that little puddle of water in the bed.

Breathing is difficult. Memories come back to me in three dimensions with their colors, smells and tastes. The cold preserved all their freshness as if I were seeing this fruit or that red bicycle for the first time. The sapodilla with its velvet peel so soft to the touch. The yellow-eyed dogs wandering through the night. The little girls jumping rope while screaming in voices so high-pitched they sound like a flock of birds. The old man at the window of the big wooden house by the Paramount movie theater. The plume of smoke on the mountain. Things today replaced by others of the same density, so that every traveler can make himself a store of images and emotions he can recover at his return.

I also remember the picture
in the living room in the house in Petit-Goâve.
A little uninhabited island
overgrown with fruit trees
where young felines played together.
That's where I spent my afternoons
when things got too heavy for my young life.

Intolerable heat.
A white bowl filled with water
in the shadows of the bedroom.
Three mangos next to it.
I eat them all, bare-chested.
Then wash my face.
I'd forgotten what mangos taste like at noon.

I go out on the veranda.
A great coconut palm
planted right in the middle
of a house under construction
is dancing in the furious wind.
I watch the scene from the hotel balcony.
For a war correspondent,
that's not much action.

This city awakens so early
that by two o'clock in the afternoon
it's on its knees.
In the shade of their broad hats
the ladies who sell melons
are taking their nap.
Their backs against the hotel wall.

Their voices so shrill they break your heart
the women hawking baubles
desperate to sell off their trinkets
and the aggressive horns of the drivers
going from the office to the restaurant
can't quite cover the lullaby
this woman is softly singing to her daughter
sleeping between two sacks of vegetables.

I receive an urgent summons to the phone. I slip on a pair of
pants and rush down to the reception desk. It's a guy who says
he's a childhood friend of mine. All he wants is money to pay
his daughter's hospital bills. I hesitate but he tells me he's just
on the other side of the gate, calling from a cell phone. I'm
about to go looking for him when the receptionist motions me
to forget it. "I know the fellow, he always tries that with my
guests," she lets on with a wide smile.

I've been away so long I can scarcely remember the faces
that flash past me so quickly, demanding to be recognized.
"Don't you remember me?" A feeling of shame. "Your cousin
introduced us the night before you left." So we met once, thirty-
three years ago. I'm alone in the middle of eight million people
with shared family and personality traits jammed onto half an
island, and they all want me to recognize them. They all come
with a story that I'm a part of. Apparently we once went to the
movies together, forty years ago. I was the best friend of that
guy's older brother. Surely I must know the cousin of the other
guy who lives in Montreal. My head is spinning. Sometimes I
put a voice to a face but they don't belong together. It took me a
while but I understand that in this thirst to be recognized, they
are looking for confirmation that they're not dead.

I was paging through
the paper on the couch
when I noticed his shadow
pacing in front of the gate.
Now I don't dare go out.

Through the Window of the Novel

The hotel owner points out that all the information in today's paper is at least a week old. For the news of the day, you're better off with the radio. The delay, in an area in which the ability to deliver information rapidly is more important than the information itself, acts as a buffer between the event and ourselves. That way we're protected from the bad news, which comes to us with a few days' lag. By the time it reaches us, the shock wave has been absorbed somewhat by the dense sweating crowd. These few days between the event and ourselves are enough to maintain our equilibrium.

The news of the week concerns both the upper-class neighborhoods and Cité Soleil. A rare occurrence. A young man "from a good family" who'd been kidnapped several months ago has become one of the country's most pitiless gang leaders. The family's lawyer declared on the radio that "he didn't want to get kidnapped anymore and that's why he became a kidnapper." In the poor districts they're still laughing about what the editorialist called the "Stockholm syndrome." The answer wasn't long in coming: it appears in graffiti painted on the walls of Cité Soleil. If a rich kid who gets kidnapped by a gang becomes a gang leader after two weeks because of the Stockholm syndrome, then how come a criminal who spends years in prison doesn't become a cop when he gets out?

We learn that most kidnappings are carried out between people who know each other well   sometimes they belong to the same family. That's where hatred is most deep-rooted. That's where everyone knows the exact amount of money the victim has in his bank account. The ransom demands become more precise and there's less negotiation. Kidnapping has become such a lucrative business that the rich weren't going to miss out on the action for long. Unlike the photos of the hoodlums at the young man's side, the paper took the trouble to blur his picture.

Since the government can't throw impertinent journalists in jail the way it used to, the upper classes have picked up the slack by buying them off at rock-bottom prices. They buy off the corrupt journalist with money. They buy off the poor but honest journalist with considerations. They buy off the perverse journalist by letting him breathe in the subtle perfume of the very young woman who leans toward him during a classy cocktail party.

I just saw the vendor
who wakes me up every morning.
Her high-pitched voice rises above the rest.
I can still hear her when I come back in the evening.

The newspaper vendor who works in front of the hotel tries to get me to pay the price of a whole monthly subscription for one issue. I show him my photo on the front page. He's not impressed and names me the same exorbitant price. I grab a copy from his hand and give him fifteen gourdes. That's the price people who live in gourdes pay, he snaps. How do you know I'm not from here? You're at the hotel. That's my business. For me you're a foreigner like any other foreigner. How much do you ask from people who go by in their fancy cars? He walks away, muttering. It's a good thing the newspaper vendors only read the headlines. Otherwise we'd be prisoners of the fifth estate.

That banal incident
makes me limp
as if I had
a stone in my heart.

To be a foreigner even in the city of your birth.
There are not many of us
who enjoy such status.
But this small cohort
is growing ever larger.
In time we will be the majority.

Climbing the gentle slope
that leads to Saint-Pierre Square,
suddenly I think of Montreal
the way I would think
of Port-au-Prince when I was in Montreal.
We always think of what's missing.

I wander into a new bookstore called La Pléiade. At the end of
the '60s, I used to go to Lafontant. He was always sitting by the
door: an affable man despite the bushy eyebrows that gave him
a surly look. He didn't speak much. We would go straight to
the back to look for the books that interested us—never more
than one at a time. We chose them from the famous Maspero
collection, which was censored by the paranoid powers of the
day. Old Lafontant took a chance selling something besides
detective novels and trivial magazines displayed on a table by
the entrance. We calculated the price and, moving past the cash
register, put the exact amount on the counter. Without a look
back, we made our way to the exit. The entire operation had to
be carried out seamlessly. We would practice at home.

We would get together afterward,
my friends and I,
in our little restaurant
across from Saint-Alexandre Square,
each of us with the book he'd bought.
We would put all the books on the table.
Then draw straws to see who would read what.

We were so serious at twenty
that a girl practically had to rape me
before I understood
what was happening around me.
The girls who listened to The Rolling Stones on the radio
had already progressed to the sexual revolution
while we were still reading the New China News Agency.

We were desperately seeking
in the speeches of our idol Zhou Enlai,
that severe, elegant Party strategist,
the scent of a woman
the glimpse of a leg
or the downy nape of a neck
that would have given us the gift
of erotic dreams.

I opened my eyes and realized we were just a tiny group busy
making the revolution in our minds, which mainly meant com-
menting on the political essays we purchased at Lafontant's
store. The rest of the world lived in carefree pleasure and was
no worse off for it. I was ready for my first intellectual vacation.

Suddenly I was terribly attracted to the very guys I'd had such
contempt for a short time earlier. Guys who lived for dressing
sharp, wearing the right cologne and dancing to slow songs by
The Platters. Guys who'd never opened a book. And who didn't

care about the feelings of those inaccessible princesses who filled our dreams, but only about their graceful slender bodies under their Saturday night dresses. Guys into whose arms those princesses melted, the ones who never considered us. Guys whose bloody faces on page one of the newspaper (they always ended up in a fatal sports car crash) got more press at the Girls' College than Davertige's latest volume of poetry.

Old Lafontant bequeathed his bookstore to his two daughters (Monique and Solanges) who split it into two parts. One store in Port-au-Prince, a little bigger than the one in Pétionville. I converse a while with Monique who runs the Pétionville branch. She points to a girl paging through one of my novels. I am fascinated by the back of her neck (the nape speaks volumes about a woman reading). I go into the courtyard, under a tree, to keep from embarrassing her in case she turns and recognizes me. I never imagined that one day I'd find myself at La Pléiade as a writer.

As I move through this universe (the city, the people, the objects) that I've described so often, I don't feel like a writer, but more like a tree in its forest. I realize I didn't write those books to describe a landscape, but to continue being part of it. That's why the newspaper vendor's comment hit me so hard. In Port-au-Prince at the beginning of the seventies, I became a journalist to denounce the dictatorship. I was part of the little group that bared its teeth to power. I didn't ask any questions about myself until that sexual crisis at the very end. I grew aware of my individuality in Montreal. At minus thirty, I quickly developed a physical sense of myself. The cold lowers the mind's temperature. In the heat of Port-au-Prince the imagination is so easily enflamed. The dictator threw me out the door of my own country. To return, I had to slip in through the window of the novel.

The Red Jeep

The crowd pushes me into the street.
Cars brush past me.
I'm already running with sweat.
Suddenly a red Jeep stops next to me.
The door swings open.
I get in.
A second later I'm not part of the prey anymore.
My friend drives through the crowd.

He saw my picture in this morning's paper.
He called *Le Nouvelliste* and his friends
to find out what hotel I was staying at.
No one could tell him.
And now, just like that, here I am in his car.
He gets on the phone to his wife.
You'll eat with us?
I nod yes.

In the red Jeep with chrome wheels.
The music loud.
We talk over it.

On the side of the mountain
a small yellow airplane skims the treetops.
The pilot sticks his head out the window to wave
to the young boy who pulls off his shirt as he dances.
My childhood cuts through me like a knife.

My friend and his insouciance are just like before.
Here, he tells me, we live intensely
since we can die at any time.
Those who live in the lap of luxury
speak most casually of death.
The rest are simply waiting for death,
which won't disappoint them.

The women descend in single file.
Along the cliffs.
Mountains of fruit on their heads.
Their backs straight.
Their necks sweaty.
Elegant in their effort.

A truck breaks down
on the narrow road to Kenscoff.
The women climb down.
The merchandise is already on the ground.
The men have to push the truck
onto the side of the road.
A low chant rises up.
The voices of men working.

The higher we climb, the fewer people we see.
That brightly colored little house
on the mountain is
hidden in the morning fog.
Settle in there and write
that long historical novel in five volumes.
Mistaking myself for Tolstoy late in life.

The red earth produces such beautiful onions.
The vendors hoist their baskets up to our level.
My friend lowers the window to buy
carrots and onions.
The smell of rich earth makes me dizzy.

The voices of the peasants
coming down the river.
Barefoot in the water.
Straw hats.
Each with a fighting cock under his arm.
And a bottle of alcohol
in his back pocket.
They are going single file
to the Sunday fights.

A dog looks for a sunny spot
then ends up lying down by the wall.
Its muzzle moist.
Its eyes half-closed.
The siesta comes early.

Everything grows here.
Even what no one has planted.
The earth is good.
The wind scatters the seeds.

Why do people gather
where it smells of gasoline and shit?
Where it's always too hot?
Where it's so dirty?
Even as they admire beauty
some prefer to live in ugliness,
often richer in contrasts.

I can't breathe
when the air is too pure.
The landscape too verdant.
The living too easy.
The urban instinct is sharp within me.

From the other side of the cliff,
a horse slowly turns in my direction
and casts a long look at me.
Even the animals have started to recognize me.

Maybe that's what a country is:
you think you know everyone
and everyone seems to know you.

The Jeep swings suddenly to the left.
For ten minutes or so, we follow
a narrow unpaved road
then come to a farm with a green roof
in the middle of wide fields.

My friend's wife, a tall redhead,
is waiting for us at the door.
I have the feeling, in front of this Irish flag
hoisted in the pasture among the cows,
that I'm in another country.

Some time after I left Haiti,
he went to Ireland
where he lived for twenty years.
He brought Ireland back with him
to this green hamlet set upon
the heights of Pétionville.

When I was in Ireland, he said to me, I lived as if I were in Haiti.
Now that I'm in Haiti, I feel totally Irish. Will we ever know who
we really are? That's the kind of question that makes us feel
intelligent even under a blazing sun. Such vanity is no match for
a second rum punch.

Like a flight of wild birds
we left almost at the same time.
We scattered across the planet.
Now, thirty years later,
my generation has begun its return.

We talk underneath the mango tree, with so much passion,
about the years abroad: a whole life. His wife listens with a tired
smile as she sips her coffee. She has come to sit with us. Her
only demand is that we speak Creole when she's around. The
language touches me here, she says, pointing to her round belly.

As she walks me to the car, while her husband goes to give
orders to the staff, her voice is determined. I'm going to make
sure my child's mother tongue is Creole. If mother tongue
means the mother's language, then it'll be English. No, it's the
language the mother chooses to teach her child: I want to raise
him in Creole.

I decide to tell her a story. Back in Petit-Goâve, when I was
eight years old, I met a woman who came from some unknown
place. She was white and walked barefoot through the dust
of Haiti. She was the woodworker's wife. They had a son my
age who was neither black nor white. I never understood how
someone could live in a culture other than their own. Despite
the thirty-three years I spent in Montreal the mystery remains.
As if I were talking about someone else.

In that little room in Montreal,
I read, drank wine, made love
and wrote without fearing the worst every morning.
But what can I say about this woman
who came from a free country and chose
to live in a dictatorship?

She tells me this story.
One of her girlfriends who lived all her life in Togo
and who she asked for advice before leaving Belfast
explained to her that people are not necessarily
from the country where they were born.
Some seeds are carried elsewhere by the willful wind.

My friend comes back. He kisses his wife's neck; she squirms
and moans under the sun. Nothing is more sensual than a pregnant woman. We get into the Jeep and circle the Irish flag before
coming back to her. She moves toward the door. They smile at
each other with their eyes. She touches his forearm. He starts
up the car again. She stands in the sun a while before going
back into the house. If ever he gets it into his head to return to
Ireland, she won't go with him.

A Little Cemetery Decorated Like a
Naïve Painting near Soissons-la-Montagne

Already we're at the stop, at Fermathe,
where they sell grilled pork
and fried sweet potatoes.
A truck full of people eating.
The anticipation in the air
before the long descent
into the deep South.

It takes as much time
to travel to another country
as it does to go from one city
to another in this country
over the broken roads
and along the edge of dizzying cliffs.

We run a gauntlet of screaming vendors
who jam their fruit baskets in our face.
Laughter rises above the racket.
A man's impertinent remark.
The sudden gaiety of the women.

The driver slows down
and all the men lean toward
the singing river far below
where bare-breasted women
are washing the white sheets
of the rich ladies of Pétionville.
A colonial scent.

Where is that young girl going, seething with rage
through a field of yellow flowers
that lie flat as she passes by?
The ability of a girl that young
to produce such anger just might be
the palpable sign that this country still has
some guts.

A woman, under a mango tree,
offers us a coffee.
The river isn't far.
The air is so gentle
it hardly brushes my skin.
The music of the wind in the leaves.
Life is weightless.

A little cat
looking for its mother
finds a dog
of the tolerant sort.
Now both are sleeping
among the flowers.

We get back on the road and find ourselves behind
a long row of cars
full of men wearing ties
running with sweat
and women in black.

The cortege stops
at a modest cemetery decorated
by the local peasants.
Where did they get the idea
to paint death in colors
so brilliant and with motifs so naïve
they make children laugh?
For the naïve painter
death is as ordinary as the sunrise.

A visit to the painter Tiga
who lives close by the cemetery
that so impressed Malraux.
Thin as a reed.
Head like an insect.
Bristling with intelligence.
He sits down, gets up, goes to the window and returns
with an idea so natural
it seems simple.
And what's rare for a mind so inventive:
other people seem to matter to him.

The peasant painters have come together
under the banner Saint-Soleil.
Daily life in this village where people spend
most of their time dreaming and painting
revolves around the solitary star
that so intimidates Zaka, the peasant god.

My life has been adrift since that late-night call
announcing the death of a man
whose absence shaped me.
I let myself go knowing
that this wandering is not in vain.
When we don't know the destination
all roads are right.

The Jeep stops
near the Pétionville market,
the very place
where we met this morning.
At length we embrace,
without saying goodbye,
feeling we won't be seeing each other
again soon.

Tropical Night

I feel as if I know that man sitting on a bench in Saint-Pierre Square, the little plaza by the hotel. He seems so absorbed in his reading. His hair has grayed, but he has that familiar way of stroking his cheek with his fingertips. He is the only person I ever saw read poetry in an algebra class. He was drinking in *Alcools*; a single verse of it soon had me inebriated. I went to his house and stayed until I had read all the poetry books in his father's library. His family read nothing but poetry. Without ever wanting to write any, as his father said proudly. I touch him on the shoulder. He raises his head and without as much as a smile makes room for me next to him. He is still reading Apollinaire.

His father died in prison. They destroyed his library, supposedly because it concealed communist books. The man who hated communists because he suspected them of not liking poetry suffered a blow to the head and died of a cerebral hemorrhage a few days later at the military hospital. My friend wasn't at the house when the regime's henchmen visited. *Alcools* is the only book that wasn't destroyed that day because he had it, as always, with him—he never weaned himself off Apollinaire. And he never wanted to leave the country despite the appeals of his uncle who lives in Madrid and reads nothing but García Lorca.

He is working as a proofreader for the book pages at *Le Nouvelliste*. Just enough to survive. He could have been a literary critic, but he'll have nothing to do with other people and reads but a single poet ("humble as I am who am nothing worthwhile"). He still lives in the little room he had when I first met him. He closed off the other rooms the day a friend who works at the palace informed him of his father's death. Ever since he's been adding alcohol to poetry. He works at the paper in the morning and spends his afternoons reading on this bench, waiting for nightfall.

Night falls so suddenly in the tropics.
Night black as ink.
Surprised by the darkness all around me
I walk behind the man slowly
reciting Apollinaire.
The smell of ilang-ilang
uses the darkness
to spread over
this poor district.

We slip silently between
two rows of lamps.
The melodious voices
of the women whose silhouettes
are sketched upon the market walls.
Their sung stories were my childhood lullaby
on summer evenings.

The indolent gait
of a cow
on her evening stroll.
The night becomes
a Chagall painting.

Those nubile young girls from the poor parts of town
wearing flimsy sandals slip like geishas
over the asphalt still warm from the sun
on their way to the movie house near the market.
Soon their lovers will meet them.
Young tattooed bandits they kiss
all along their way.

Before I left, that sort of thing didn't exist, working-class girls who kissed in public. The only films were the ones the government bothered to screen ahead of time. The authorities established a morals brigade that spread out through the parks looking for unmarried lovers. They were married on the spot. The inspectors demanded, when the captive was worth it, to try out the goods first. The government figured that the more virtuous the population, the less likely it would rebel.

Raucous voices.
Near the nightclub.
On an out-of-the-way street.
Three pickup trucks crammed full
of peasants in Sunday clothes
come to town for a wedding.

The fragile napes
of the young women
contrast with
their calloused hands.
Our hands always reveal
our class origins.

The laughter of these one-night beauties
in the perfumed night
lets the young tiger on the prowl
locate them easily.
Then choose one,
bring her back to his lair
and devour her at his leisure.

A half-naked woman
preparing for the evening
at the end of a long corridor.
Car headlights
sweep across her glowing breasts.
To protect them from the eyes of predators
she quickly covers them with her hands,
revealing her swelling sex.

His father would spend his evenings at home. He died, he
believes, never having known the night. We climb slowly
toward the square. I watch him now that there's light to see.
He brushes close to people, takes in smells, savors the moment
as I have rarely seen someone do. Worried that his precious
knowledge of the night will one day disappear along with him,
I ask why he doesn't record his nocturnal adventures in a collection of poems or a personal journal. With a weary wave of his
hand he lets me know he has no desire to share such emotions.

A pack of dogs ready to fight for a bone that a passerby just
threw them. They break into two groups. The bone between
them. Suddenly each goes for the throat of the other with
no care for the bone. I turn to make a comment about their
behavior, which doesn't seem much different from humans
but he is gone. Faded into the night that has suddenly grown
opaque. I go back to the hotel and hope for sleep.

A swarm of little yellow-and-black motorbikes
like bees in search of pollen
buzzing around Saint-Pierre Square.
So it really is the end of Papa Doc's
sharks in dark glasses.
New barbarians are in town.

A Generation of Cripples

From the hotel balcony, I look onto the square,
the marketplace, the bookstore
and in the distance the dusty road that leads down
toward my mother's house.
Besides the excursion with my friend to his farm
I have not left this secure perimeter.

What is frightening me? Not the Tonton Macoutes who have
melted into the population since Baby Doc's departure, afraid
of being discovered by someone they once tortured. Not the
young guys on motorbikes who descend like locusts on this
neighborhood of hotels and art galleries frequented by the few
foreigners who risk visiting the country. I don't stray far from
this golden circle; I don't want to feel like a foreigner in my
own city. I keep putting off that moment of confrontation.

When I was a teenager, Pétionville was the rich suburb we
visited on Sunday afternoons. In Saint-Pierre Square we hoped
to spot upper-class girls out for a stroll. Things have changed
since then. The rich have sought refuge on the mountain.
To find out what life is really like, I should go down to Port-
au-Prince where a quarter of Haiti's population is squirming
like fish out of water. For four decades the landless peasants, jobless people and wretched of this nation have been
converging on the city.

I think of my mother who
has never left her neighborhood.
I think of those six million Haitians
who live without the hope of leaving one day,
if only to catch a breath
of cool air on a winter's day.
I also think of those who could have done it
and haven't.
Then I feel badly looking out on my city
from a hotel balcony.

Near Sainte-Anne Square I meet an old friend I haven't seen
since I was a teenager. At the time he lived in this workers'
neighborhood where he still lives. What amazes me most since
I've been back is how almost no one has left their district. They
have gotten poorer but keep fighting the wind that wants to
blow them into more miserable quarters.

I remember the neat square with the flowering bushes
surrounding a tall statue of Toussaint Louverture on horseback. Right across from the school of the same name. Now
the bushes are black with mud. People's faces gray and dusty.
Houses with filthy entrances. I don't understand how people
can get used to such calamity.

I promised myself not to look at the city
with yesterday's eyes.
Images from the past constantly try
to superimpose themselves on the present.
I am navigating through two worlds.

Sometimes we used to follow the train to filch
bits of sugar cane and chew on them
in the shadow of the King Salomon Star.
That crummy hotel became a bordello at night
while during the day it served as the headquarters
for all sorts of wildlife from the countryside
who'd come to the capital to do their dirty deals.
The real traveling salesmen stayed
in a modest hotel near Martissant.

We would lie down on the rails and jump out of the way just
before the train came. We'd bet on who would get off the track
last. My friend won every time. One day I asked him what
his secret was. I close my eyes, he told me, and imagine I'm
making love to Juliette. Juliette drove us all crazy back then. Of
course he'd want her to be his. I wouldn't have gotten off the
track in time. I meet him again: he is a prisoner of his wheelchair. He can't move his legs. First I thought that desire had
won out over fear. Once he told me that after his friends left,
he would go back and play this Russian roulette all by himself.
Can you play that sort of game alone? Who's the winner then?
That was his way of having an orgasm. The closer the train
came, the clearer Juliette's face would become.

   We lived in an electric atmosphere. It was dangerous just
to stick our noses outside when the sharks in dark glasses
paraded past in their luxury cars with young Dominican
prostitutes smoking long menthol cigarettes. Often a machine
gun pretended to sleep on the backseat. They spent whole
nights gambling at the casino. We had to stay out of their way
when they went home at dawn to sleep, because they didn't
think twice about firing at anything that moved—just to play
another game. Their primary job was the Chief's security.

They'd invent some political plot just to throw their weight
around in a recalcitrant neighborhood.

My friend got shot in the hip at the casino
by an officer jealous of the way his wife
couldn't take her eyes off him.
The story got into the papers.
The President offered him money.
His father refused.
The opposition wanted to make a hero out of him.
He refused.

I watch him concentrate all the energy
he can summon on the thing
that stokes his desire.
He begins to burn
when a girl in a short skirt
brushes against him not suspecting
the effect of such provocation
on a man in a wheelchair.
He can't move his legs
but the organ in question
still seems quite alert.

I'm afraid to call the roll
to find out what state
my generation is in.

Some work for the government, others are in prison. Some
vegetate, others live in luxury. Some still go in for seduction,
others have aged prematurely. But those who never could leave
the country and who always wanted to, feel, when they meet me
again, that it's up to a new generation to dream of that journey.

In Praise of Diarrhea

I went by the pharmacy and on the glass door there was a
message scrawled on a piece of cardboard: "Closed for Funeral."
Diarrhea had kept me up all night. I couldn't stop shitting,
amazed once again at how much the belly can hold. The night
before, I drank some fruit juice from a stall along my way,
just to prove that I was still a son of the soil. Nationalism can
trick my mind, but not my guts.

The young pharmacist with icy hands
recommended Buscopan
and amoxicillin three times a day.
Next door I bought a bottle of water
and began the treatment immediately.

I run to the hotel bathroom and settle in comfortably. I might
be in for quite a stay. I look around and on the window ledge
I discover an old issue of *Historia* that tells me everything about
Himmler's ascension through the Third Reich and the court
rivalry, at the end, when they were done in like rats in the
bunker. It was understood that the war was lost when Nazi offi-
cers started dressing without first taking a shower. I thought
of my teenage years, when those stories fascinated me, which
threw my mother into despair since she was scared silly of
everything that had to do with politics in any form. Strangely
she stopped worrying about me once I published my first article
in *Le Nouvelliste*. It was a long literary commentary about *Ficus*, a
novel that had just come out. In any other country, literary criti-
cism would not have been a dangerous vocation, except for the
risk of getting slapped by a parlor poet offended by some unflat-
tering comment about his latest volume. But not in Haiti. My
article provoked two reactions that were decisive for my career.
The first came from Professor Ghislain Gouraige, the author of

the monumental History of Haitian Literature (from independence to the present) that we studied in school, and who congratulated me for the originality of my opinions even as he pointed out a dozen errors of fact. That was followed the same day by a summons to the barracks of Major Valmé. According to established criteria, I had arrived.

My mother, trembling but determined, accompanied me to the office of the fearsome Major Valmé. I was exceedingly calm. The Major called for a coffee for my mother but did not allow her to attend the interrogation that was to be "a friendly conversation between two true lovers of literature." My mother insisted, but the Major asked a non-commissioned officer to look after her. All this kind attention, instead of reassuring her, only increased her anxiety. But the conversation with the Major went well and did not go much beyond the subject of literature. As for the novel by Rassoul Labuchin, his opinion differed from mine. For him, Labuchin's real project was not literary but political. Did I know that the author had spent time in Moscow? And that he was the confidant of the communist writer Jacques Stephen Alexis? In my opinion, General Sun, My Brother by Jacques Stephen Alexis is one of the most beautiful novels in Haitian literature. Quite spontaneously he replied that his preferences leaned toward Romancero aux étoiles. Mauriac was his favorite writer. Mauriac's description of the bourgeoisie of Bordeaux reminded him of his own adolescence in the provinces. He ended the conversation by congratulating me on my "clear and readable style so unlike the usual Haitian manner." I was impressed by the man's elegance and culture, though I did not forget that he ran Papa Doc's torture chambers. At times we heard screams coming from nearby rooms. Still, I continued to believe that literature would save me from all harm. On our return, my mother, too overwrought to ask me what was said in the office, took me out for a sandwich and a Coca-Cola and even wanted to buy me cigarettes. I wrote a literary column in the weekly *Le Petit Samedi Soir* until my colleague Gasner Raymond was murdered by the Tonton Macoutes on June 1, 1976, on the beach at Léogâne. I went into exile immediately afterward, in Montreal.

Learning of my intestinal misadventures
the hotel owner advises a rigorous diet.
I should stay in my room for the time being.
If only to be close to the bathroom.

Bored with the prison of my room,
I go down to the hotel bar.
A little tv perched on a shelf
is broadcasting the funeral of that young musician
killed last night in a car crash.

People are no longer used to
death by natural causes
if a spectacular collision
can be considered
as a natural not a political cause.

I read in the paper
that there were five of them in the car
but we'll remember the one whose
fiancée killed herself when she heard the news.
To remain in popular memory
events must have brutal connections.
Love riding on death.

It's true I pay attention only to the
apocalyptic images that cross my field of vision.
I don't listen to rumors and I'm indifferent to ideology.
Diarrhea is my only involvement
in Haitian reality.

From time to time the old servant woman, not as old as the
owner but more workworn, brings me a very bitter liquid to
drink. The older the women are, the more unpalatable their
remedies. The owner whispers to me to pour it down the sink
and go on taking my medicine. She recommends rest—the
country won't disappear in a week. How can I explain to her
that time has become an obsession for me? We are not living in
the same time frame even if we are in the same room. The past,
though it defines how we make sense of the present, does not
have the same weight for everyone.

I turn in circles in this room.
My security perimeter
is shrinking ever smaller.
I'll write a book about life
around the hotel.

A man by the hotel entrance
looks at me a while
though he can't quite remember who I am.
He reminds me of someone too.
It takes us five minutes to
bring blurry images from the past to the surface.
To think we were inseparable at one time.
We smile, then say goodbye.
As if we had never seen each other.
The only way to preserve the little that's left.

This narrow street
was a wide avenue
in my memory.
Only the thick bougainvillea bush
remains the same.
I used to hide behind it
to watch Lisa who
I was already in love with.

I notice that some details
change into emotion
depending on the color of the day.
I see yellow like a drunk man.
That's the state of someone with a fever too.
I make myself a rum punch and lie down.

In the darkness, I feel a hand on my forehead.
I pretend to sleep.
The two old ladies are close by.
They evaluate the situation.
Nothing too serious.
The fever has broken, one of them says.
I hear them go slowly down the stairs.

Galloping Rain

Suddenly the first raindrops fall and everyone runs for shelter
under the marquee of the Paramount movie house. For a while,
the guy at the ticket counter must think that Godard has
become the star of Port-au-Prince. Once the danger passes, I am
the only one who stays to watch *La Chinoise* in the giant theater
filled with red staved-in seats.

After the film, I want to walk in the rain.
Up ahead, kids dance
naked under a curtain of water.
The rain gallops toward me.
I hear its music.
An emotion that rises up from childhood.

I go to those kids
playing soccer
in the rain.
Time is fluid.

It's not that easy
to be in the same place
as your body.
Space and time united.
My mind begins to find rest.

Recovered is the primitive energy
I thought I'd lost
and the wonderment
I felt so long ago
watching the red top
that consumed my childhood
as it turned so fast before my wondering eyes.

Early in the morning
the little girl tries
to light the fire
to make the coffee
that will begin the day
for so many.

We climbed and climbed
the flank of this deforested mountain.
Our necks sweaty.
Noon beating in our throats.
Then at the summit, we discovered
the sea languorously
stretched out along the bay
like a courtesan
on her day off.

Nature immobile.
The sky
the sea
the sun
the stars
and the mountains.
I'd see the same thing
if I returned in a century.

I stand for a while
in this fine drizzle,
my face lifted to the sky.
Naked children from nearby streets
come and encircle me
as if I were a strange apparition.
I speak to them in Creole but that doesn't work.
Their astonishment keeps me at a distance.

That's when I understand
that speaking Creole is not enough
to become a Haitian.
In fact it's too vast a name
to apply to real life.
You can be Haitian only outside of Haiti.

In Haiti people try to find out
if they're from the same city
the same sex
the same generation
the same religion
the same neighborhood as others.

Those young boys who danced naked
in the rain, I decide
as I go back to the hotel,
did not want any adults to join their game.
Childhood is an exclusive club.

A Carefree Young Woman

I arrive at the hotel completely soaked and find my sister deep
in conversation with the owner. We go up to my room so I can
change. She stopped by after work to check up on me because
my mother was starting to worry. In a dream she pictured me
in some danger. That's because now I'm in her sensitive zone.
During the years I spent in Montreal, she never seemed so
concerned as she is now when I'm only ten minutes away. You're
wrong, my sister tells me, she's been worrying ever since you
left. I'll go see her tomorrow. My sister isn't fooled by my mother's subtle emotional blackmail. She knows her well. She has to
come home at the same time every day, otherwise my mother
gets it into her head to go looking for her in the streets of Port-
au-Prince. How do you search for someone in a city of more
than two million? My mother does just that. And nine times out
of ten, she'll find my sister.

One of my aunts told me that back when my father was still
there, my mother was a carefree young woman. Capricious even.
She lost her job after her husband left. She expected as much,
but she always thought she'd find something in the private
sector. But the dictator had erased the line between public and
private. There was nothing but Duvalier, everywhere. Even
behind closed doors. People whispered that he could hear what
was being said in the bedroom. All territories belonged to him.
That was the beginning of my mother's long descent. It took
decades of anxiety, frustration, humiliation and daily struggle
to turn this proud and resistant woman into the fragile, worried
little bird she has become.

My father always wanted my mother to join him. Despite
her wild need to see him again, she did not want her children
to grow up in exile. She wanted to give us a sense of country.
One night when I was sleeping near her, I heard her murmur

in a soft voice that she'd love to touch his face one last time. My father's features were imprinted on her retina. She missed the weight of his body. She held fast for nearly half a century, divided between her man, her children and her country. She had all of them at once for only a brief time.

I can't seem to have a personal conversation with my sister. We understand each other too well. I can follow the arc of her life even if I don't know the events that shape it. Our relationship moves between the closeness of our adolescent years and the distance forced on us by exile. A good deal of that oscillation is due to the fact that we didn't spend our childhood years together. She stayed in Port-au-Prince with my mother, while I was sent to my grandmother's in Petit-Goâve. We spent our nights telling ourselves stories. We go about it differently. She tells; I analyze. I give importance to a minor event by tying it to a chain of events that are just as minor. I believe that stories aren't necessarily big or small but that they're all linked together. The ensemble forms a hard and compact mass that we can call, for convenience's sake, life.

My sister and I form a single person. The only thing we can't share is my father. I've always suspected her of hoarding images of my father in action. If anyone could remember his face, it would be her, even if she's a year younger. I was in Petit-Goâve when my father was in Port-au-Prince. He lived with my mother and my sister in a big wooden house on Magloire-Ambroise Avenue. My sister was three years old and I was four. She's always maintained she can remember my mother's voice when she was nursing her. And I've always been the only one in the family who believes her. As for me, I remember nothing, except what my mother has told me. Knowing my sister's exaggerated sensitivity to detail and absolute olfactory abilities,

I'm willing to bet she remembers my father's smell. We can't speak of his death because we shared nothing of his life.

Aunt Ninine takes me aside. She carefully closes her bedroom door. We stand in the middle of the room. Suddenly, she attacks. You have to save Dany. I have to save myself from what? I'm talking about your nephew, you have to save Dany. From what? You have to do something for him. I don't understand. He has to leave this place. We decide people's destinies here? He's twenty-three years old but his opinion doesn't count. His life doesn't belong to him. He absolutely has to leave this place, my aunt repeats. What's the point, I think, if it only means returning thirty-three years later like me? My mother comes into the room wearing her mischievous smile. Aunt Ninine immediately begins talking about her health. My mother can feel that something is going on and she leaves us to our discussion. I head for the door to escape what's coming. Just as I'm about to cross the threshold, Aunt Ninine grabs me by the arm. Something tells me that, even if my nephew's future is important for her, it is not her only concern. Zachée called about your father. Your mother needs your support now. Even if he did disappear, your father was the only man in this house. Her way of blaming me for my absence these last few days, or would that be the last three decades?

Can anyone know what goes on in the head of a man who has lost his mind? I wish I'd inherited his ideas of social justice, his intransigence toward power, his disdain for money and his passion for other people. And what would your mother get? What she was always able to hold onto above and beyond her pain. Our eyes meet in silence. Then Aunt Ninine finally opens the door.

The Killer on the Motorbike

In the theater of Port-au-Prince
everything comes at you live.
Even death which can show up
at any moment
on a Kawasaki.
Death imported from Asia.

A young man in dark glasses
revving his little yellow Kawasaki
shows off on the square.
"A bad seed," declares
the lady sitting next to me.

We find out later
that a young man on a motorbike,
without even stopping, shot at
two doctors
going into their clinic.
Right close by.
Death at top speed.

The witness (a man of about sixty): "I was right there, next to the doctors who were talking. I heard a motorbike. I turned around to see where it was coming from. Bang. Bang. Two shots. The two doctors fall. One's shot in the throat, the other in the heart. He didn't even stop."

A crowd quickly gathers around the only witness to the two murders. The ambulance hurries to pick up the wounded. One is already dead. The other who was shot in the throat doesn't stand much of a chance. His wife rushes up and starts talking about having him transferred to Miami by helicopter.

The same witness: "I admire people who are good at their job. He hardly slowed down at all. Such precision! Not every-body can do that, I mean, I rode a motorbike for ten years. It was a Kawasaki, a new model. Compact but reliable. Obviously if you've got a bike that breaks down, as often happens, then it's more risky. You can see he takes his job seriously."

A policeman comes up to him. The crowd parts in front of the man who is still admiring the killer's precision work.

Policeman: You're coming with me.

Witness: Why?

Policeman: You seem to know what's going on here. I think you're going to be able to help us.

Witness: I happen to live around here... I'm just a motorbike fan.

Lady: Maybe he likes motorbikes but he doesn't live around here. I've been in this neighborhood for forty-six years and it's the first time I've seen him.

Policeman: You're going to come with me.

Witness: I live in Jalousie, just up the mountain.

Lady: All the hoodlums who terrorize us live up there.

Witness: I'm not an accomplice... I simply appreciate a job well done.

Policeman: Come with me or I'll put the handcuffs on you.

Witness: This is a democracy...

Other Lady: Maybe he's telling the truth, maybe he just likes motorbikes ... Some people don't know when to keep their mouths shut. When faced with death, we must simply bow our heads.

Policeman: Come with me. And you, Madame, you're a witness too?

First Lady: No, I was eating when it happened.

Policeman: All right, break it up, move on, everybody ...

When everyone
runs every which way through the market
it means there's someone
for whom time has stopped.
Lying on the ground in his own blood.
The last spasms of life.
The sound of a motorbike speeding off.

The young guy on the bike got away easily.
But they'll catch up to him soon enough.
The slum where he lives is crawling with
police informants
most of whom are killers too.

According to a *New York Times* investigation most of the murders are ordered by powerful businessmen who live in the luxury villas high on the mountain slope. Right across from the slums where the killers live.

The contracts are negotiated by cell phone, from one ghetto to the other. The starving masses and the upper classes have always been interested in technological progress. The latter for security reasons. The former to remain in the battle.

Near the University

Since I'm here I take a look around. I like to scout out the locations and know where I am, to avoid ending up in a blind alley if ever I have to run. I come across a little park filled with former students who can't find work. Those who haven't yet understood that only ten percent will get a decent job when they get out of school. And that their studies aren't enough. To work in this country, a bitter but lucid student told me, you have to come from a good background or ally yourself with a powerful political family.

The unemployed lying on park benches
with white handkerchiefs over their faces.
A few prostitutes in miniskirts
trying to pass themselves off
as modern literature students.
A dozing policeman,
his gun and nothing else between his legs.
Rest for the wretched.

A girl accompanies her mother
who is herself so young she could
be her older sister.
They accost me quickly
to inquire after my desires.
They say that a mother and daughter in the same bed
can still excite an old senator.
I'm not there yet.
They go off with their arms around each other's waist.
From behind, I can't distinguish the mother from the daughter.

The young man sitting next to me watches the van full of police from the international squad go by. The more cops there are,

the more thieves. What do you mean? I ask. They're all the
same. I don't get it. The ones who are supposed to be protecting
us are in business with the killers when they're not killers themselves. How do you defend yourself? We walk in the shadows
and stay at home as much as we can. I'm telling you only a
dictator can save this country. How old are you? Twenty-three.
I bet you never knew the dictator. No, but I'm telling you all the
same: this country needs a leader, otherwise it's total disorder.
And where is the chaos? He gives me a stunned look. I see order
everywhere. The powerful keep everything for themselves.
Since the little guys have nothing, they tear each other apart
for the few crumbs that are left. If we name a dictator, we'll
simply make the way things are official. I still believe we need
a leader in this country. These days, every neighborhood is
controlled by armed gangs that constantly fight each other and
terrorize everyone else in the process.

We take a few steps into the park. What are you studying?
Political science. And you want a dictator? Yes, sir, anything
but this untenable situation. We could always protest against
the dictator on the international scene or even try to topple
him. The one I knew, if you add the father's regime to the son's,
ran from 1957 to 1986, twenty-nine years. What you're seeing
now is their legacy. A dictator would only give them legitimacy.
And order serves only to enrich one particular group. Disorder
begins when other groups start demanding their share. You
don't live here? I came from Montreal. And there's no dictator
there if I understand correctly. No, but there's winter. It's not
the same thing. Of course not, I was joking. His face darkens.
Is the winter so terrible up there? You have to go through it
to understand. So it's subjective then? More like democratic.
Everybody suffers. Not everybody: those who can get away, do.

It's like here: people who have the means don't have to suffer the rigors of dictatorship. I'd like to go up there and see one day. You don't just go and see. You go for a while and end up spending your life there.

I leave him, hoping he won't end up like the people he is denouncing. Still, he's got the right profile. The feeling of being looked down on by a certain class, the enormous financial difficulties that keep him from satisfying his most primal needs, and to that you have to add an immoderate taste for flowery language and the loneliness (sexual hunger is part of it) of someone who was orphaned at an early age. Not so different from the young François Duvalier when he wrote his poem "Les Sanglots d'un exilé" whose main theme is the resentment that would later serve as his political platform.

I continue my walk
trying to remember
the dictator's poem I had to
learn by heart at school.
"And the black of my ebony skin was lost
in the shadows of the night.
When, that night, as hideous as a madman,
I left behind my cold student room."
Everything is there. Frankenstein let loose.

At the far end of the park, there is a small market where the ladies selling tea entertain themselves with no heed for the few customers. One of the women is telling a sex story with all the appropriate gestures. She shakes her big round butt in the youngest woman's face to tease her. The other women look on and smile, their heads resting on sacks of tea. Now and again laughter rises in the perfumed air.

A skinny young man
tries to load a long rifle
while slipping on a khaki cape.
His friend also plays the role
of security guard in a supermarket
across the street.
A city ready for war.

Crazy about rap music.
Reads only mangas.
Eats only pasta.
Quiet by day.
Talkative by night.
That's my nephew.

We understand each other easily.
Looking at him I think of those times
when everything exasperated me.
I avoid preaching to him
and slip him some money
when his mother is looking elsewhere.
Money is to boys
what perfume is to girls.
It makes them euphoric.

The young woman at the cash in this little restaurant near
the university has a way of smiling at me. A few students are
wolfing down a mountain of rice. The old waiter ambles over
with our plates, his shuffling feet barely leaving the floor.
Everyone has the same meal (chicken in a sauce, white rice and
potato salad). We eat with our heads down. A tall glass
of soursop juice. Close by, my black notebook where I write

down everything happening around me. The smallest insect visible to my eye.

If there is one thing I like about my nephew, it's how he isn't in a hurry to talk. He hasn't opened his mouth since he got here, but when he does, it's for real. That part of town isn't too dangerous? Sometimes it is. When the government decides that we're too quiet, it sends in agents disguised as students to stir things up. How do they do that? They show up a week before the police. They start by recruiting the leaders. Then they wait for the right time. We know they've started their game when on a Monday morning tires are burning in the courtyard of the school. Then the government sends in a squad of cops to supposedly restore order. The tv is in on it too. Standing at the windows, the provocateurs pretend to fire at the police hidden in the park. They end up wounding one or two of them but never seriously, which gives the squad the excuse to charge. Five minutes later, the tanks arrive. What do you guys do? At first, nothing, we sucked it up, but finally we figured out their technique and invented a little system that so far seems to be working. As soon as we see the flaming tires, we slip away and let them face off against each other. They fire at one another thinking we're still in the area. Luckily they're pretty stupid, but they'll end up catching on sooner or later. His calm even voice frightens me. He seems unimpressed by what could happen to him. No more than a slight smile that reveals a subtle appreciation of the facts. In any case, he continues, I don't know why they go to such trouble to screw up our plans when nobody wants to stay here anyway. If they don't want us around, they should just hand out American visas and the university would empty out in a minute. The students seem even more desperate than in my day. Still, that was Duvalier. The Tonton Macoutes.

The black years. The bloodthirsty police force of a barbarous regime. The bitterness may well spring from the fact that they believed a change would come after Baby Doc's departure. Nothing worse than hope betrayed.

I always dreamed of living on a campus back when I was in Port-au-Prince. My main activity would have consisted of assiduous library attendance because of that girl who was doing research on the slave trade and its impact on the European economy of the period. I would have participated half-heartedly in the interminable discussions about the Wajda and Pasolini movies screened by the film club at the back of the yard. And in the accusation of censorship leveled against the rector who would have prevented the first-year students from watching *Deep Throat*. And in stormy protests against the government that would have confiscated the copy of *State of Siege*. The first kiss with the girl from the library the evening before a major exam. The feeling of having to choose between her and my future. And of screwing up my life no matter what choice I made.

The Ancient Caribbean Wind

My mother takes me aside
to give me a little photo
of my father with my sister on his lap.
And me standing beside him.
My sister is crying.
My father and I have the same serious face.

My mother tells me the photo was taken by a friend of my
father's, a "comrade in arms." They tried to take another
picture to have a happier memory of that sad time, since my
father and his friend had made a quick visit before heading for
the hills, but my sister wouldn't stop crying all afternoon.

Her voice becomes even softer as she remembers that
afternoon. My father's friend was called Jacques. He was so
full of life. He played guitar and loved to dance. After the
photograph, he played a Spanish song in fashion at the time
and my mother danced in the kitchen. Since my father and
Jacques were being hunted by the President-for-Life's men,
they disappeared once night fell. Later my mother found out
that Jacques had been caught and had died in prison.

People who have lived under several regimes change
mood depending on whether they are remembering happy
or unhappy periods. The happy periods, like tropical rains,
are intense and short-lived. They are often followed by long
tunnels in which no one sees any light for decades. When my
mother looks at today's young people dancing in the streets
after a government falls, she gets sad, knowing they will
soon change their tune. But as she always says, "at least
they got that much."

My mother is looking for something in the armoire.
At the very back I see
a large black-and-white photo
of a young man who looks like me.
It's the only photo I've seen of them together
at the time they met.

When I look at this photo, my mother says,
I feel like I'm with my son and not my husband.
The last time she saw him
he was still in his twenties.

My mother asks me how I managed to survive back there. Her
question comes as a surprise since it's the first time she has
come so close to the edge of the precipice. I seem to be leading
a good life, but my mother isn't interested in whether I've
succeeded or not. Her question is about how it happened. How
what happened? Then I understand she isn't expecting me to
describe the obstacles I faced in order to make a way for myself
in my new country, the usual business you tell journalists. She
wants to know how I felt about it. She's waiting for my answer.
It's a question I've long avoided, and coming here is a way of
finally facing it. Only a mother would insist on descending into
an abyss like that with you.

I might have been ten years old.
I had just left my grandmother
to come live with my mother in Port-au-Prince.
For the first days I slept with her
until they bought me a mattress.
My mother had a toothache.
I heard her whimpering very quietly
for fear of waking me up.
These days when I tell her to take some medicine,
she replies that a small pain
keeps her from thinking about the larger one.

My sister comes back from work.
Everyone wants something from her.
She escapes by disappearing into the bathroom
with a magazine.
We hear her turning the pages.
The family waits for her to come out
so they can devour her whole.
This insatiable appetite for attention.

I go out on the gallery to be with my mother. Her universe, so
dreary at first sight, is actually very rich. She knows the two
birds that meet here every afternoon, at the same time. She has
named the lizards after her dead brothers and sisters: Jean, Yves,
Gilberte, Raymonde, Borno, André. Dead or in exile. That way
I can remember their names. Otherwise I forget a name, then
the face that goes with it. That's how you lose a part of your life.
She even has a name for the wind, this gentle breeze that comes
to rock her to sleep when it's time for her nap. If you're quiet, a
new world appears. Little things take on life. Sometimes she is

eager to join them. Other times her anger with life is so strong she refuses that illusion. She will stay in her room for a week. Finally, she comes out, and all those things are there, waiting for her return, patient as always. She tells me they don't show themselves unless they feel our despair.

The Death of Benazir Bhutto

The death of Benazir Bhutto comes to me while I am in the
bathroom. The final spasms of on-and-off diarrhea. From
another room, I hear the high-pitched voice of bbc's female
correspondent in Pakistan repeating the name Benazir Bhutto.
In general, when someone speaks the name of a public personality more than three times in a sentence, that person has just
died and the death was violent. Before the journalist's commentary comes to an end, I hear a series of explosions. Screaming.
Sirens. A terrible uproar. I can't move because my diarrhea has
returned with a vengeance. The noise of the crowd covers the
journalist's voice. I imagine at that very moment, all around the
world, people are feeling the same sense of surprise, though
no death was more predictable than hers.

It's strange that the Middle East
in a certain way gives the impression
that the dice aren't always loaded in politics.
People still risk their lives there.
All that anyone risks losing here
is their reputation.

What moves me
in this story of bloodshed
is the return of Benazir Bhutto
for her funeral,
to her native village of Larkana.
We always return in the end.
Dead or alive.

The wooden chamber.
Benazir, who wanted
to run a vast and populous country,
must feel cramped in there.
And very alone in that room
though it was made to measure.

We're born somewhere.
If we can
we take to the road.
See the world, as they say.
Spend years out there sometimes.
But, in the end, we return to our point of departure.

The Wild West

Coming back to the hotel, I pass five kids straddling a low
wall under a mango tree. They are playing cowboys and Indians.
Four decades ago I was one of the Indians. We would rush
down the hill, brandishing our tomahawks. The cowboys were
waiting for us, hiding behind their stagecoaches. At the last
moment they would shoot us down in full stride, like birds.
One afternoon, I refused to show myself in plain sight like
a fool, since the Indians knew the terrain better than the
cowboys, and there was no reason why they wouldn't use their
experience. I was immediately made a cowboy. An Indian who
protests becomes a cowboy. I understood there and then that
being a cowboy or an Indian simply depends on how the guy
organizing the game feels. Or who is telling the story. There's
no use complaining about the role we're given; we just have to
take the one we want. These little frustrations, accumulated
over the years, end up erupting one day in bloody revolt.

A friend stopped by unannounced,
and we talked all evening.
That's quite a change from life up North
where everything is arranged by phone.
If we eliminate all surprise from life
we strip it of all interest too.
And die without realizing it.

I seem to think
everything is good here
and everything is bad back there.
It's just the swing of the pendulum.
For there was a time
when I hated everything about this place.

Men can't hide anything
for long.
Observe them
and they will strip naked before you.
A cocktail of sex and power
and soon they're dead drunk.

I'm holed up in my room, fascinated by the documentary
I already saw once with my nephew. It's running twenty-four
hours a day on a local channel. Besides the violence, what
makes the story successful is its clarity. Dazzling sunlight,
dusty streets and two brothers ready to cut each other's throats
for the love of a woman. A real western. At last death has found
an esthetic form.

Bare-chested, wearing jeans.
Gun in hand.
Close-up on Tupac.
The young prince of Cité Soleil.
His carnivore's laugh must arouse
the girls as they watch
cloistered in their wealthy manors
high on the mountainside.

Rarely does a local legend
get us interested
in faces
and not just landscapes.

Here come the final images.
The music that tells you the end is near.
Death at the end of the day that will turn
these young men into heroes of the Cité.
The story takes me back to the beginnings of this country
when our heroes went barefoot
in the golden dust of twilight.

In the distance I hear that irresistible music.
I picture people drinking,
flirting, dancing and laughing.
Who could imagine that not far from the party
a man lying on his back
is seeking out his path through the Milky Way?

At fifty-six, three-quarters of the
people we've known are dead.
The half-century is a difficult border
to cross in a country like this.
They move so quickly toward death
that there's no sense speaking of life expectancy.
It should be death expectancy instead.

If the bullet goes wide.
If even hunger spares you.
Disease won't miss its mark.
All three together if you are
the chosen of those perverse jesting gods
who grimace in the darkness.

In my early evening sleep
I wonder where that sports car is going
at full throttle through the darkness.
The triumphant roar continues as far as the wall
of the blind alley.
If my ears serve me well
a wealthy young man has just met
that implacable god his father's
money could never buy off.

I am here watching
what I have seen before,
even without having seen it,
and dwelling on what I already know.
A strange sense of immobility
in the midst of my feverish activity.
Is this what the cat feels
just before it leaps?

An old doctor, a former minister of Public Works I met at a gallery opening, invited me to his house in Kenscoff, on the heights of Pétionville. We have been driving through the darkness for a while now. A well-maintained Buick 57 is the Rolls-Royce of the Caribbean. I am Gérard of the Gang of Four, he says, turning in my direction. I was a very close friend of your father's. My blank look reminds him I don't know much about my father's life. And he is not at all surprised. The four of us were inseparable: your father, obviously, Jacques . . . I've heard of him. Of course, he says, sad suddenly, he was the best one of all of us. My mother liked him. He was Marie's friend, but your mother kept an eye on me. Why is that? Since I had a lot of girl-friends, she thought I'd introduce one of them to her husband, but Windsor had his own stable. And the fourth was François. Is he dead too? No. He's holed up in the countryside. That guy was so brilliant and now he's some kind of peasant. There are times when I don't understand this country, as if we all had a suicidal virus. We just can't seem to enter modernity. You think you know a guy because you've seen him every day for years and suddenly he announces he has to return to the shadows because a household god is demanding his presence there. Is that what happened with François? I don't know if it was some kind of voodoo business, but in his case, what a waste! Where does he live? The last time I came across him, it was in Artibonite. He was involved in growing rice. I was on my way to Cap-Haïtien when I saw a peasant up to his waist in water. I told my driver to stop. The peasant was François. And to think the guy could have been minister of Agriculture in any government. I did everything in my power to bring him back to Port-au-Prince, you can imagine, the guy loved Brecht and Genet, but to each his own path. Monsieur François is in Croix-des-Bouquets now, the chauffeur says. I know, the ex-minister replies with a note of irritation, I've been told he's raising chickens. The Buick 57 speeds through the night. The chauffeur seems to know every pothole in the pavement. He avoids them with such dexterity it's like driving on a perfectly paved road.

As we get close to Pétionville
the girls seem younger.
Their skirts shorter.
Their gazes more meaningful.
This war is as ferocious
as the one between the Cité Soleil gangs.

Girls have always paid
a higher price when the city
turns into a jungle
and the night becomes a trap.
A hungry cock
spares no one
in its path.

Though the hour is late, we detour onto the Delmas road to go see Frankétienne. The doctor wants to buy a painting in his latest style. Frankétienne is so prolific an artist he can ruin a collector. He welcomes us so uproariously he must have woken up the whole neighborhood. The ogre in his lair. Despite the doctor's rich praise, Frankétienne is reticent about selling him a painting from his personal collection. The rich doctor lets him know money is no object, but the painter digs in his heels. Coffee arrives—Frankétienne hasn't touched alcohol since his illness. Right now he is working on a novel whose voluminous manuscript stretches across his wide worktable in spectacular disorder. Everything is larger than life with him. Bare-chested. Gargantuan appetite. Face as red as a boiled lobster. The wild enthusiasm of a man obsessed with literature and painting. He has painted several thousand canvases and his first great novel, *Ultravocal*, has metastasized into some thirty volumes over forty years. Urban turbulence is the only setting for this ogre. Seeing how perplexed I am by this expanse of paper scribbled with obscure signs that look more like musical notes than letters of the alphabet (I wouldn't put it past him to invent a new vocabulary and grammar in order to write a truly original book), he announces that his next work will be an opera-novel. What's an opera-novel? asks the chauffeur who seemed to be dozing in the corner. Frankétienne turns to him abruptly: you're the first one who ever dared ask me that question. Everyone else pretends to understand. I can't explain it, but when I finish the book, you'll see, and in the meanwhile, allow me to give you a painting. He disappears into his storehouse and returns with an enormous canvas we'll never be able to get into the car. He disassembles the frame with such energy he nearly rips apart the painting. He throws it into the trunk of the Buick 57 as the doctor-collector looks on in astonishment, empty-handed, his pockets still stuffed with money.

On the highway a desperate woman waves at us to stop. The doctor orders the chauffeur to drive on. Apparently it's the bandits' latest trick for robbing travelers. She's the bait, and the thieves are hiding in the thicket. But what if it was true? If she really did need help? I'll read about it in the paper.

For the scene to be believable
they kidnap a poor woman
and promise to set her free
if she manages to trap
one of those luxury automobiles whose owner
has a villa on the mountainside.

In Le Nouvelliste I read about the tragic story of a woman who
ended up by the side of the highway after an accident, with her
son. No one wanted to stop. The boy bled to death. Months
afterward, the mother, having lost her mind, was still asking
motorists for help. Even the murderers who have set up shop in
this desolate region avoid her. They're afraid of looking her in
the eye.

For every hand that points
a revolver at you
another hand will offer you a fruit.
The hateful words of one
are erased by the other's smile.
We can't seem to move
between these two extremes.

How Do You Live at Seventy inside a Museum?

We leave the lights of Pétionville behind.
Already there are peasant huts
lit by lamps
the wind is trying to blow out.
What I need
is a little room
with a window
from which I can see the green countryside.
There I could write the book
I have been ruminating on for so long.

We drive down a road made of ocher earth
and stop at the red gate.
The servants arrive rubbing their eyes.
Three cars, in lieu of farm animals,
are sleeping in the yard.
The doctor, his wife and their numerous domestics
are the only ones living here.
The children have scattered across the planet.

This man lives in a veritable museum. Three salons filled
with works by major Haitian painters. The pioneers: Wilson
Bigaud, Rigaud Benoît, Castera Bazile, Jasmin Joseph, Préfète
Duffaut, Enguerrand Gourgue, Philomé Obin and even a Hector
Hyppolite. Then the generation of Cedor, Lazare, Luce Turnier,
Antonio Joseph, Tiga, and contemporaries like Jérôme, Valcin,
Séjourné, and the Saint-Soleil group with Levoy Exil, Denis
Smith and Louisiane Saint-Fleurant. An entire room is devoted
to Frankétienne. Almost everyone is there. The doctor follows
behind me, smiling. I'm impressed by the choice of painters,
and the choice of certain works intrigues me just as much. And
even more so the way they are hung. I can hear their dialogue

in the night. Why no Saint-Brice? He lowers his eyes. My wife
is afraid of Saint-Brice. Most of Saint-Brice's paintings are of
heads without bodies, and they frighten my wife. I did own a
small Saint-Brice that I had the misfortune of putting in the
bedroom. My wife woke up in the middle of the night, saw the
picture shining in the darkness and started screaming like
a madwoman. I took it down immediately and put it in the
hallway, but that was worse. She refused to leave the bedroom,
even to go to the toilet. I had to exchange my only Saint-Brice
for two Séjournés. It's hard to imagine what a collector feels
when he has to give up a major piece. Well, I had to get rid of it.
Shall we have a drink?

We move into the small salon—a figure of speech because it
is much bigger than any normal room of its kind. Two servants
magically appear bearing plates loaded down with cold cuts.
I like the rich when they know how to receive guests. Food:
cheeses, ham, pâté, smoked salmon. Drink: rum, wine, whisky.
I don't dare ask him where the wealth comes from. I know
what you're thinking. If you were my father's friend, then how
could you be rich? He begins to laugh. We never knew if we'd
have anything to eat back then. But your father managed to
overcome even the most difficult obstacles. He knew how to
get himself invited by rich women who are always intrigued
by insolent young men. Your mother suspected me of pushing
him into the arms of other women. But he was the seducer, and
like any good seducer he never tried to seduce. Sometimes he
wasn't even aware of the chaos he created along the way. How
many times did I have to point out to him that some woman
was feasting on him with her eyes? But he had politics on the
brain—for him, that meant getting his ideas out into the world.
For him, women were just potential party militants, though

they were bewitched by that powerful energy he gave off. His incandescence attracted us. I saw things, but I suppose that's not what you want to talk about . . . I don't expect anything. I'm happy just to listen to someone who knew my father when he was twenty. Your father hated General Magloire for clinging to power despite the Constitution: that was the basis of everything. Either we were in prison or hiding out in the country. And then? The results, like everything our generation did, were disastrous. Jacques died, your father went into exile and François retired to the country. I was the only one who stayed, and guess what you do in Port-au-Prince? You make money. No, he said, smiling, not so fast. First we were in politics. The revolution, you mean? We made the revolution when we were twenty. A pause. For fifteen years I was minister of Commerce; that's a good place to make money. Most of the merchants downtown are smugglers who shower the minister with gifts so he'll turn a blind eye to their clandestine operations. I closed one eye and kept the other open. Because those same merchants won't think twice about denouncing you as soon as things get a little hot.

Later, he escorted me into his office for a serious discussion. Since the latest riots, no one trusts the domestics any more. Unlike the rest of the house, his office is almost monastic. That's where he plots his master strokes. He moves his armchair close to mine so our knees touch. He pours himself a shot of rum and fills my glass to the brim. Let me explain a few things to you that you don't seem to understand, which is normal for someone who's been away for more than thirty years. You may think we're living under a new regime since the one you knew isn't operative anymore, and its children are all overseas. But they've been replaced by their former enemies who are a lot worse than they were. They are frustrated and starved, and they panic at the thought that they might not be able to devour everything before they croak. But really they're just puppets that other people are manipulating from behind the scenes. We never see the true masters of this country. For them, the story has been running without a break. A single straight line. They've been keeping watch over things since the end of the colonial period. It's always been the same business: one group replaces another, and so it goes. If you think there's a past, a present and a future, you've got another thing coming. Money exists; time doesn't. He takes a long sip of rum and gazes at me through bloodshot eyes. I'm going to do something for you because Windsor was my best friend. I'm going to let you have my car and my chauffeur so you can move around the country in complete security, since you haven't seen the place in a while. I'm falling asleep on my feet. Now, if you'll permit, I will go off to confront my childhood monsters.

The Men Who Thought They Were Gods

I decided to bring along my nephew
who was bored silly
in a house
full of nervous old aunts
and rosaries blessed by drunken priests.

I see a lot of pregnant women.
An endless flow of newborns
insidiously urging
the old folks toward the cemetery.
Always keep a black jacket close at hand
after you hit fifty.
You'll need it to attend the funerals of childhood friends.

The open gate of the art center
where I spent time when I was seventeen.
More for the painters
than the paintings.
This morning there is no one but Mademoiselle Murat
who's been the director forever.
She greets me with mocking eyes
softened by a disarmingly guileless smile.
She has lived so long among paintings
that she's become a character in a novel.

I tour the dark empty rooms
of the art center feeling as if the tenant
has just left without daring to take along
the many paintings that come to life
in this wooden building with creaky floors,
as I drink a cup of coffee
served by Mademoiselle Murat
with the disturbing but warm-hearted Robert Saint-Brice
and the big baby-faced boy named Jean-Marie Drot.

I should write a story from the point of view of the dog
wandering through the purple painting by that painter
who disappeared one day without a trace.
That was back when a man was no more than
a rabbit in Papa Doc's black hat.

I realize as I go by a small crowd praying
that people here talk about Jesus
in a normal everyday tone,
as if he were
someone they could
always meet
on the street corner.

They expect everything of him,
but in the end settle for very little.
The slightest surprise is welcomed
like a miracle.

Mental stability depends on being able
to move, without a transition,
from a Catholic saint to a voodoo god.
When Saint James refuses
to grant a certain favor
they quickly direct the same prayer
to Ogou, the secret name given
to Saint James when the priest began enjoining
the faithful to renounce voodoo
in order to enter the Church.

If they accept the gods so easily
it's because people believe
they are gods themselves.
Otherwise they'd be dead already.

In those places where people tell each other
their dreams every morning
over the first cup of coffee,
turning day into a simple extension of night,
the traveler wonders if this sense of tranquility
in the face of death springs from the fact that
time is not used to measure life here.

That little girl, not even nine,
feeds her younger brother
and goes without food herself.
Where does such precocious maturity come from?

A Man Sitting under a Banana Tree

I used to like going to Jean-René Jérôme's little studio in the
crowded suburb of Carrefour. I would spend hours watching
him paint women with lovely curves and a red flower behind
their ear, which he did to support his bohemian lifestyle.
He worked very quickly, with scarcely a glance at the canvas.
Since we weren't far from the sea, at noon we would go eat fish
on the beach. Years later his wife sent me a small photograph
of him and me drinking coffee in his studio, packed with paintings, seashells and dusty sculptures. Today he looks so young
in the photo. I can't remember what we talked about. I just
remember my pleasure as I watched him dance as he painted
those lighthearted, sensual women. As for the paintings that
really mattered, he would hide in order to paint them.

That fog in the distance
is rain moving in on us.
Chaos already. People running everywhere.
How is it that people
who on a daily basis
face disease, dictatorship and death
panic when it comes to getting wet?
I treasure the radiant face of the peasant
walking into the rain.

We stop by the side of the road for this old gentleman who
seems to be returning from mass. Where are you going?
I'm going to see a sick lady friend, just at the bend of the road.
Climb in, you'll get there faster. I'm almost there as it is.
I insist, and he gets into the car. I'm not used to automobiles.
I consider I'm an automobile myself, he says, laughing at his
own joke. Sure, but sometimes they can help if you're in a hurry.
I don't see what could make me go faster than my own two

feet. You can leave me here. I watch him climb a little path snaking upward. I bet he's going to the other side of the mountain, the chauffeur laughs. When he reaches the top he'll still have another good hour's walk. Why didn't he tell me where he was going? His world is not ours.

If we return to the point of departure
does that mean
the journey is over?
We won't die as long as we're moving.
But those who have never crossed beyond
their village gate
await the return of the traveler
to figure out whether it's worth
the trouble of leaving.

The poor peasants pay taxes
without expecting anything from the government.
Things would be all right
if it let them live in peace.
The State doesn't like being judged in silence.
I think of that as I see them bent over in the fields.

Near the old Port-au-Prince cathedral, I bought a magazine that had a long interview with Lazare the painter. He spent a good part of his life in New York before returning to Haiti. After a very brief stop in Port-au-Prince to say hello to a few friends, he moved on to the little hut tucked away on a banana plantation. The image of that place, almost religious, brightened his loneliness in New York. He awoke one morning in a sweat, with the feeling that his last day in this hard, cold city had come. He knew he would suffocate if he didn't return immediately to Haiti. He grabbed his passport, emptied out his account at the Chase Manhattan Bank and took one final taxi ride to jfk. That evening, he was back in a small café in Pétionville with what was left of the old gang of painters and poets who once dreamed, as he had, of changing the world at the beginning of the sixties. But his journey wasn't over, and wouldn't be until he reached the hut that had kept him alive during his long years of depression in New York. In the magazine photo, Lazare sits bare-chested under a banana tree; in the background is a little thatched hut with blue windows.

We've been driving blind for a while.
A truck is raising a great cloud of white dust
ahead of us.
A long line of trucks
carrying sand stretches out behind us.
Blaring, urgent horns.
We roll up the windows to keep from swallowing
that penetrating dust.

After a few hours of driving, we have to pull over to the side of the road. Smoke is pouring out from under the hood. The chauffeur leaves with an empty can to get water from a peasant who lives on the side of the bare mountain. Water, so rare in this dry region, is offered to us even before the chauffeur can ask. The peasant says he will come down with his family to help us push the car. The chauffeur spends the evening cleaning every grain of sand out of the motor. Night falls. The man offers us a place to stay. We climb the mountain holding each other by the hand to keep from getting lost in the darkness.

The house where we sleep
has no roof.
I spend the night strolling through the Milky Way.
And I think I recognize my grandmother
in a lonely star
I spot for the first time,
not far from the Big Dipper.

A Window on the Sea

Bare mountains on the right.
Giant cactus on the left.
The asphalt road from a distance
looks like a quiet lake.

The trucks that used to carry
animals to the slaughterhouse
are now used for humans
who travel standing,
their heads covered with dust,
their mouths filled with mosquitoes.

We near the famous cliffs
that provoked the
worst nightmares
of my childhood.
Reality is much more modest.
At the bend the blaring horn
of a red truck coming in the opposite direction.
Childhood fears surface again.

You have to wonder whether the country's highways aren't
all one-way because the peasants who travel to Port-au-Prince
never go back. First they are sucked in by the center of the
metropolis, then they're soon thrown back toward the overcrowded periphery. Where it is impossible to survive without
at least a knife.

Beyond a certain number
people's lives don't have the same value.
They're used as cannon fodder
or they do the dirty work.
Some manage to make a way for themselves

without being too compromised
by general corruption
and everyday murder.

We arrive late in Ville-Bonheur where
two virgins reign.
The Christian one is called
Mary of the Immaculate Conception.
Her twin, who sits on the throne in the voodoo pantheon,
is Erzulie Freda Dahomey.
Thirsty virgins.
One, for blood,
the other, for sperm.
The chauffeur pays tribute to both.

At the end of the road
we find a small hotel,
completely rickety,
where food is being served.
The bedbugs are waiting for us between the sheets.

How can we convince this woman
who is so proud of having been to New York
that all we want is fresh fruit juice
and not warm Coca-Cola?
For her, the local fruit is good only
for poor people and pigs.

The young man who seemed
so dangerous with his scarred
face turns out to be sweet-tempered.
His wounds were caused
by a thief he caught in his field.
As so often happens we
confused the victim and the criminal.

Everything is a miracle
in this little place.
Starting with the mere fact of existing.

A pig made it possible
for the young man to study agronomy
in Damien, near Port-au-Prince.
He speaks of it like a member of the family.
The pig is the peasant's bank account.

When after an epidemic
they asked the peasants in the region to kill
all the pigs to avoid putting
people's lives in danger
they hid them in the mountains.
In the eyes of a peasant a pig
may be worth less than his family
but certainly more than the advice of the minister
of Agriculture.

We stop at a snack bar by the sea. Thatched roof. No door.
Everything exposed to the elements. Six bare tables. The sea
literally beneath our feet. On the menu: grilled fish, salted fish,
threadfin in hot sauce. My nephew can't abide fish. The chauffeur and I tuck in. He even agrees to loosen his tie.

I watch my nephew eating oysters with his face to the sea. From time to time a truck goes by, without stopping, its passengers covered in dust. The feeling that in this country you don't go from one city to another but from one world to another. The horizon is completely empty. Except for the lady selling coconuts who is at the mercy of the truck that stops sometimes, but few of them do at this time of day.

Just as we get back in the car
we change our minds
dive naked into the warm sea
and stay there
till nightfall.
The chauffeur sits on the hood of the car
and waits patiently.
The strange poise that men in the tropics have.

I felt
I was
lost to the North when
in the warm sea
in pink twilight
time suddenly became liquid.

My Father's Other Friend

Return to Croix-des-Bouquets where, this time, I catch up with
the painter I used to see all the time before I left. He is a skillful
colorist who used to paint nothing but landscapes filled with
pigeons and overripe fruit. We talk a little and drink a lot in his
darkened studio. Rum for me. Milk for him since his illness. A
bunch of bananas rotting in the shadows reminds us of his odd
obsessions. His heavy body. His sleepy voice. We slip into lethargy. The fact that the studio is also a voodoo temple adds to
the paintings' poisonous charm. The strange way of looking he
has and the enigmatic way he speaks put me ill at ease. I always
feel we are communicating between two parallel universes:
the master of this place and me. Once we leave, the chauffeur admits he felt strong negative vibrations in the room. My
nephew had spent the whole time watching the young vendors
in the yard next door.

A large basin of cold water
where young women selling mangos
bathe as they cover their breasts
and scream in shrill voices.
Their dresses plastered to their bodies.

The painter emerges from his studio
to show me the road
that leads to my father's friend.
He lives, he told me, behind the market.
We had to make a long detour.
It is impossible to drive through the market.

The chauffeur parked under a tree
then went to look at the stalls.
Some malangas had caught his eye.
My nephew stayed with him.
I have to meet my father's friend by myself.

I find him feeding his chickens. He seems even more frail than
in the photo I saw at the ex-minister's house. His piercing eyes
and firm handshake tell me it would be a mistake to under-
estimate him. A strong personality. He goes and fetches two
chairs and sets them under the arbor. So he's dead. Who's dead?
I ask like an idiot. Your father. He recognized me. Someone
told you. I don't see anyone besides my chickens and the peasants who come and ask me to write letters for them. How do
you know then? You're his spitting image. And that's the only
reason you'd come all this way to see me here. You want something? All I drink now is tafia. I'll have a little glass too. In this
heat it's not advisable for someone who comes from the cold.
Something cool then? He nods discreetly to a girl washing
clothes under the mango tree. That's my granddaughter, Elvira.
Since her mother died she lives with me... So, Windsor K is
dead. He died in Brooklyn. I don't give a damn where he died.
You don't die somewhere, you just die. He retreats into memory
for a moment. Our history teacher had to absent himself for
one reason or another, and Windsor took his place. He got up
in front of the class. And immediately demanded silence from
the bunch of stubborn mules that we were. Then he told us
the history of our country, according to him. We all sat there,
stunned. Never seen anything like it. He was seventeen—we all
were. I watched him go through his paces and I said to myself
that I'd follow that guy anywhere. And that's exactly what I did.
I wasn't the only one, but I was the closest to him.

Elvira comes back barefoot
in the warm dust
with the drinks on a little platter.
Piercing eyes.
A shy smile.
Long graceful legs.
Her modesty can't
hide the explosive energy
she got from her grandfather.

We drink in silence. I couldn't have said what my drink is
made of, but with an effort I recognize papaya, grenadine,
lemon, soursop and cane syrup. In any case it's cold. I look
around as I listen to the voices of the mango vendors. We're
in no hurry here, he tells me with a mocking but friendly
smile. Windsor knew a lot of people, but we were the Gang of
Four. The inner cell. What we wanted was simple: revolution.
Windsor got the idea to start a political party. We were twenty
years old. "The Sovereign," because it was the party of the
people and the people are always sovereign. We didn't follow
any rules. We had no qualms about using our fists. We went into
the offices and kicked out the pencil-pushers and replaced them
on the spot with honest and competent employees who didn't
necessarily belong to our group. We had one list of dishonest
employees and another list of competent, honest citizens who
couldn't find work, which meant we had plenty to do putting
things right. We didn't have a job; we had a mission. We wanted
a country run by citizens, not cousins. We were for action.
What about Jacques?

Elvira comes back with a basin of water
and places it on a rickety little table.
François gets up to wash his hair,
his armpits and his torso.
She dries him tenderly
with a big white towel.
The young vestal virgin
caring for her grandfather.

His face transfigured now. Suddenly he's twenty years younger.
I am a plant that needs watering from time to time, otherwise I dry out. I like water too. He sits down again. You said
Jacques . . .? Jacques! Jacques! It was like a punch in the gut and
I've never gotten over it. Neither did your father. Marie told
me because no one could know what he felt. I say no one, and
I was his lieutenant. No one except for your mother. She told
me he cried. Do you have any news of Gérard? He tosses some
grain on the ground and a few seconds later we are surrounded
by a flock of chickens. Here I will speak only of Windsor and
Jacques. You speak only of the dead? I speak only of people I
know. I thought I knew Gérard. That's all I can say. I feel it's
my turn to talk now. My father put a suitcase in a safety deposit
box. It's certainly not money—your father wasn't the type to
save. What do you think it is? I ask him. Oh, he says, scattering
the chickens, I have no idea. I have gotten rid of everything
that once weighed me down and the past was the heaviest part.
When I left Port-au-Prince, all I brought was my own corpse. But
your father was a historian; maybe they're documents, but let's
forget about it. He takes a long breath as if preparing to say one
last thing before falling into silence. All I know is that I loved
Windsor and that Jacques is the wound in my life. Now I live

here with my granddaughter, surrounded by insatiable chickens
I have to feed every hour, illiterate peasants I help to write
letters of protest, and noisy women who don't stop chattering
from morning to night, and I have all that I desire.

We leave the market area
and are already heading south
when I notice behind the car
Elvira, running in long strides,
bringing me a hen,
a gift from her grandfather.
Instead of my father's suitcase
that stayed behind in a Manhattan bank,
my inheritance is a black hen
from his best friend.

My nephew couldn't breathe
the whole time
Elvira was standing by the car.
And the silence that
followed her departure.
Like the plains after a wildfire.

A Green Lizard

I go for a walk in
the peaceful cemetery of Petit-Goâve.
Graves scattered in the tall grass.
On my grandmother Da's headstone,
a green lizard looks at me
for a long while
then slips into a break in the rock.

It isn't far from the des Vignes River
where I caught crayfish
with my cousins
during my rainy childhood.

A girl from the North came
to this cemetery
a few years ago,
with a modest bouquet of flowers for Da
whose grave she sought in vain.

That's because Da lives
in my books.
She entered head held high
into fiction.
The way others elsewhere
enter heaven.

For the simple bouquet placed that day
on the nearest grave
I promise, Pascale Montpetit,
you'll always have a spot
in the modest cemetery in Petit-Goâve,
where the gods converse
unsmiling with women.

A man napping
in the shade of a banana tree.
Lying on a tombstone
by the cemetery exit.
Is it more restful
to be that close
to eternal sleep?

I walk up Lamarre Street to number 88, the old house where
I spent my childhood with my grandmother Da. As I move up
the street, I recognize it less and less. It takes me a while to
locate the house. The little field where Oginé kept horses for
ten centimes while their owners sold vegetables in the market
has changed places. Mozart's store has done the same. Mozart
died before Da. I manage to find the house only because of the
building across from it. It has remained intact, the way it was
in my memories. The pink-and-white doors and the long
walkway where a black dog stood guard. One evening, it went
for a thief's throat.

I picture Da sitting on the gallery and me at her feet watching ants go about their business. People greet Da and she offers
them a cup of coffee. In her yellow dress, Vava goes up the street
with her mother. My friends Rico and Frantz will pick me up
and we'll go stand before the sea. That afternoon will never end.

Heading South

Just before Carrefour Desruisseaux
and the cutoff toward Aquin,
we stop at Miragoâne to
fill the car with gas.
I recognize the gas station guy.
We had our first communion together.
He hasn't changed a bit.
He's the same forty-five years later.
He still has that foolish smile that
has protected him from the sting of time.

The rain has been pelting down since Miragoâne.
An infernal racket on the roof.
We go on talking
as if nothing were happening
then quiet down as we enter Aquin.
Completely drained.
What kind of pride made us want to
challenge the fury of the elements?

The sun returns.
We come to a crossroads and don't know
whether to go right or left.
The chauffeur believes we should turn left.
My nephew thinks we should go right.
A man sitting on his gallery watches us,
drinking his coffee with his dog at his feet.
Without lifting his head, he points us in the right direction.

I'm sure on the way back he'll be
in the same spot.
In two days or ten years.
Meanwhile I keep running.
He sits unmoving on his gallery.
We will meet at least
twice in this lifetime.
On the way out and on the way back.

I am reading Césaire in the shade ("earth great vulva raised to
the sun") when my nephew approaches me as delicately as a
cat. What's it like? he asks without preliminaries. What? Living
somewhere else. Back there is like here for me now. But it's not
the same landscape. I've lost the idea of territory. It happens so
gradually you don't realize it, but as time goes by the images
you had in your memory are replaced by new ones and that
never stops. He sits down next to me with the serious look of
a young man who has started thinking too early in life. For us,
you're in the lap of luxury up there. Not exactly. Just to be able
to express yourself without fear, that's a good start. At first,
yes, it was exciting, but after a few years it becomes natural, so
you start looking for something else. A human being is a very
complicated machine. He's hungry, he finds something to eat
and right away he wants something else, that's normal, but
other people go on seeing him as the starving man he was when
he first showed up. Aunt Ninine says you're the only person
who spent three decades in North America and returned home
empty-handed. That's the way it is. That's how I am. I can't
change things. I'm one of those people who doesn't take money
seriously. I know we need it, but I'm not going to be a slave to

it. That's not what I mean! So Aunt Ninine put you up to this.
Silence. She never abandons her prey. It's all right, I'll leave
you alone with Césaire.

We go through a village that's deader than a cemetery.
Besides the mangy dog that followed us to the other side of
town, no one notices we were there. You didn't see them, the
chauffeur says, but the adults were watching us from behind
every door and the children were hidden behind every tree.
How do you know? my nephew asks. I grew up in a dump
like this, the chauffeur retorts.

Since the black hen keeps on clucking,
the chauffeur advises me
to cover her head
with a sock
so she will see nighttime
in the middle of the day.

We stop in a hamlet to buy a straw hat for my nephew who
is suffering from heat-stroke. A few huts in a half circle
around a tamped-earth yard surrounded by dusty bayahondas.
Men play dominos under a broad mango tree. A few women
are cooking at the rear of the yard. Naked children run from
one group to the other. I feel I've stepped into another time.
I didn't know that just by changing locations I could feel this
way, as if ten years separated me from Port-au-Prince, though
I've only just left it.

The Caribbean Winter

In this region
the famine was so terrible
people had to eat unripe fruit
and the leaves of young plants.
Trees stripped bare along the way.
A kind of Caribbean winter.

The sky has more stars here
than anywhere else.
The night is blacker too.
We move past people
whose voices we hear
though we don't see their faces.

Sometimes I note down
my impressions
long after leaving
a village.
Such destitution leaves me
speechless.

We drive through another dry village.
A small boy runs after the car
waving his hands wildly,
a wide smile on his face.
I watch him fade
into a cloud of dust.

I will never get over
the extreme courtesy of the peasants
who will offer you their bed
with an immaculate white sheet on it
and sleep under the stars instead.

The car stays by the bridge, watched over by a tall, serious young man who confided to me that his greatest dream is to go to Port-au-Prince one day and meet the radio announcers he listens to. The morning he spent with us, he had a transistor radio glued to his ear. When a new announcer came on, he wanted to know if we knew him. Rico? Marcus? And Bob? What about Françoise? Or Liliane? Did you ever meet Jean? He knows them intimately though he has never met them.

We climbed to the top on horseback. Of the three horses, I got the most stubborn. The one that insisted on walking on the edge of the cliff. What is my life worth to an animal that wonders what I'm doing on its back? I suffer from vertigo and don't dare look down. The young peasant guiding me gave me a knowing wink then urged the horse toward the middle of the path.

A small reception under the arbor. We are greeted enthusiastically as if we were honored guests. The people bring us coffee, tea, alcohol. There is a distillery on the plantation. A long table loaded with food. I eat the best meal of my life. Next to me my nephew shovels it in. A half-dozen girls dressed in white serve us. It's like living in a dream world where every desire comes true. The master of the property, a rich farmer, pushes me into the arms of his youngest daughter, a timid, modest beauty who has not budged from her chair underneath a calabash tree. As I get ready to go back down the path, I discover she studied medicine at Harvard, and the feast is to celebrate her return home. I like the idea of her, underneath the coffee tree, in the arms of the young peasant who is looking at her with a desire so intense he seems willing to face death to win her.

At that reception I met an old professor of Greek who was still teaching two years ago in a Port-au-Prince lycée. He had published a collection of poems in the manner of Verlaine and Vilaire. We were talking about Césaire, who left him cold, when one of his friends showed up. They began to converse in Greek. I had forgotten about culture in the provinces, so refined and so musty.

The peasants refuse to take the money I offer for their trouble and since I insist, one of them admits they have done all this for the minister. In the car, the chauffeur tells me we never would have been able to travel so freely if people hadn't recognized the minister's car. If the region enjoys irrigation, it's thanks to him.

I ask the chauffeur why he didn't eat anything at the reception. First he pretends not to hear. I have to remind him that if he fears something it is his duty to tell me, since I am under his protection. In that mysterious tone he takes on from time to time, he tells me there's no risk as long as a person knows nothing. I have to insist and finally I get a clear explanation. We were received with such respect because we represented very powerful gods. Which ones? He doesn't want to answer. And you? For the ceremony to begin, the god had to honor the meal. What kind of ceremony was it? The girl's betrothal to Legba. So I was supposed to be Legba, since the master of the house kept pushing me into her arms? No, it was your nephew. Then why did he take such good care of me? He needed to soothe Ogou, a jealous, wrathful god who could have spoiled the feast at any moment. And you? Since I hadn't taken anything illicit, I was a mere mortal accompanying the gods. I'm not sure he is telling me everything. Mystery is a vital part of voodoo. And when I hear tourists and ethnologists claim they attended "a real voodoo ceremony..." Except there is no real voodoo ceremony—it's like believing you can buy your way into heaven. The real stakes are found in other spheres.

The Son of Pauline Kengué

Monsieur Jérôme, our mysterious chauffeur who has always
refused to tell us his last name, comes from a little place that's
not on any map. One of those crossroads known only by those
who live there. Yet people are born, live and die in places like
that, just like everywhere else. No better, no worse. I discover
our chauffeur's name when we stop at the local market. People
come and gather around him, touching him with great feeling,
speaking to him gently. "I never thought I'd see you again
before I died, Jérôme," says a bent old woman selling Palma
Christi oil. For her, he is the son of Pauline Kengué, a Congolese
woman from Pointe-Noire who arrived in the village one
morning and stayed. According to the old woman who was her
best friend, the people of Pauline Kengué's tribe believe that
those who die in Africa return to earth in Haiti, preferably in a
village. Until her death, Pauline spoke endlessly about her son
Alain who had remained behind in Africa. She always said she'd
come here so Alain would feel Haitian when the time came.
We belong to the country where our mother is buried. Was
that some mad pronouncement due to the delirium of her last
moments? People will know only if the son shows up and goes
to pray at his mother's grave in this lost village in Haiti.

I can tell you that she loved you as much as Alain, says
the old woman, stroking his cheek. I remember as if it were
yesterday when Pauline came to knock on my door and show
me the beautiful baby she had found in the market. I had stayed
home that day because of a raging fever. Pauline would stop by
if she didn't see me at the market by noon. She would bring me
soup or a nice cup of clove tea. She was a good woman, serious
and honest. That day she was hiding something in a white
towel. That something was you, Jérôme. Someone set you down
in that towel right next to her. In the light of day. There are a lot

of people in a market. She thought she'd seen a woman dressed in white with a red kerchief around her neck, but she couldn't be sure. Everything happened so fast. A gift from above, that's what I told her. She called you Jérôme for her first son who died when he was three months old. That's the way Pauline was, orderly and discreet. A trustworthy friend too. Monsieur Jérôme smiles at the memory of his mother, a woman who never left his thoughts, even for a minute, or so he told us later over lunch. Whatever your age and your personal accomplishments, if people see in you the son of your mother who has long since died, it's a sign you've returned to your native village, the place of all beginnings.

Yet in the same village, someone steals our bag while we are having lunch. We had put it underneath the table, by the hen. Monsieur Jérôme is dying of shame. He keeps saying that things have changed. In his day everyone knew one another. If someone had a problem, they all chipped in to help out. They lived as a single family. So the thief isn't from here? He must come from Zabeau, six kilometers away. I know the refrain. I've heard it everywhere I've been. The cook tells us to make a deposition at the section head's office. When we get there, we are informed that he's always in Vietnam at this time of day. It takes us a while to catch on that "Vietnam" is a whorehouse on the edge of the village. Monsieur Jérôme blushes with shame again. We head there anyway. Sitting at the rear of a dim room, the section head is sipping the house cocktail, the "rarin' to go," a drink that can keep you galloping till dawn. His attention seems focused on something other than our report about a stolen bag. He keeps his sunglasses on despite the darkness. Suddenly he begins to quiver. He slams the table with his large palm and begins gasping for breath. I am about to offer him my help when a young woman crawls out from under the table, her forehead bathed in sweat. Obviously, this is not the right time to explain our problem. The chief seems ready to move on to the main course. We don't stay, despite his generous offer to share his harem.

The only way to the village of Zabeau is through a cane field. Bare-chested, sweating men. The machete whistles like an angry cobra. The first sharp blow cuts the cane at the base. Catching it in full flight, a second blow takes the top off. The stalk joins the pile a meter away. Monsieur Jérôme tells us how he used to follow his father to go cut cane. He tries, but he's lost his touch. For a moment I watch the men work, and dream of having the same dexterity with sentences. I spot figures moving in the distance. Someone is holding a secret ceremony far from prying eyes. Monsieur Jérôme asks us to get back in the car, and as we drive I hear the melodious voices of men and women singing the glory of Erzulie Freda Dahomey, the goddess no man can resist. The apparent peace of the countryside should not make us forget that these peasants have never stopped battling, first the slave traders of Europe, then the American Army of occupation (from 1915 to 1934). Today, they're fighting the Haitian government.

I have just left one of those small improvised celebrations at the side of the road. One of the few parties in the countryside that involves only mortals. In this case, the ingredients include a guitar, a bottle of rum and a few men who have been friends from childhood. The little group is making its way to the cemetery, to the grave of the guitar player's young fiancée who died at the beginning of last year. Now they are on the far side of the hill. The song is even more poignant when the one singing it is unseen.

We have been driving for a good hour when we hear a noise so startling it sounds like gunfire. Worried, people come out of their houses. A boy points at our left front tire—already flat. We pull onto the side of the road and open the trunk. No spare. "It's my fault," Monsieur Jérôme murmurs, sincerely sorry. We will have to have the flat tire repaired. Monsieur Jérôme rolls it five kilometers to the next gas station. We wait for him by the car. My nephew uses the time to go swimming in the little river at the foot of the cliff. The water is so cold it shows bluish glints. I hear my nephew laughing as he tries to catch small flying fish. Two peasants coming back from the fields watch him placidly. It's always hard to tell what they are thinking, or find out if we are transgressing a taboo. My nephew recovers the sense of pleasure his body has forgotten. You can't imagine the constant pressure that a city like Port-au-Prince exercises on the nerves of a sensitive young man.

A lady comes to offer me a well-sweetened cup of coffee, as is the custom. I drink it sitting on the car's hood. A boy who lives nearby brings me a chair. A little girl wants me to admire her skill as she spins pirouettes with her jump rope. Evening is just beginning to fall and already I hear the hum of mosquitoes preparing to attack. And now Monsieur Jérôme is coming back with the tire repaired and a swarm of children buzzing around him.

It took him a while to return because he knows a woman in the area. Attentive to the unfolding of his story, I understand they have two children together. Is she your wife? No. The children are from him, but they're not his. What does that mean? He tries to explain a highly embarrassing situation. The mystery deepens the more details he provides. If I understand correctly, his father had to acknowledge the two boys because he was a minor at the time of their birth. So they must be adults by now? His face brightens. They're good workers, and most of all they're honest. One is a shoemaker in Les Cayes, the other's a mechanic in Port-au-Prince. So what's the problem? The story is complicated, I'm afraid. The woman's father never forgave him for spoiling his plans. He had other ideas for his daughter. Her father swore he would chop off his head if he came near the house again. Even now? He's old, but he's still strong and still angry. People never forget anything around here. Monsieur Jérôme arrives at the most sensitive part of the story: he wants me to go and say hello to the woman for him and discreetly slip her an envelope. What if her father catches me and chops off my head? Monsieur Jérôme's face darkens but then he assures me that the man would never do that, since he is really quite courteous. Except when it comes to him, Jérôme. He thanks me with profuse expressions of regret for having to ask such a favor.

I doze off a little
despite my sore back.
Two nights in a row I've slept
curled up in a ball in the car.
I'd like to stretch out on a real bed.

I would have gladly accepted
the wealthy farmer's invitation to stay
if I hadn't been so afraid to end up with
his daughter in my bed, caught
in a complicated tale of dishonor
that would have been settled with one swift blow of a machete.
A necklace of red pearls.

It's not that I am
such a prize catch.
But it's an obsession among some rich farmers
to have an intellectual in the family.
The way the middle class
bought up ruined aristocrats
so their grandchildren could carry
a noble name.

Night has fallen. I knock timidly at the door. An old man shuf-
fles over to open it. Excuse me for disturbing you at such a late
hour, but I have a message for Madame Philomène. Did Jérôme
send you? he asks with a smile in his eyes. Yes. Tell him he's
welcome here. And that he can stay the night. I go back and
give Monsieur Jérôme his envelope. When we get there, the beds
are already made up. Monsieur Jérôme spends the rest of the
night conversing in low tones with his father-in-law. The next
morning, we get back on the road after a strong cup of coffee.
Suspecting that business is bad, Monsieur Jérôme does not want
his father-in-law to go to any extra trouble. When it is time to
leave, the older man declares that "this whole business was just
a terrible misunderstanding." On the road, Jérôme tells us that
the friend who was supposed to build bridges between him and
his father-in-law had lied to both of them, and that during the
negotiations he kept asking for Philomène's hand for himself,
which the old man always refused.

The Farewell Ceremony

My nephew sits down next to me
on the hood of the car.
A pink sky edged in darkness
above a vast desolate landscape.
In a moment it will appear,
bringing the world to life as we watch,
the star that novelist Jacques Stephen Alexis
called *General Sun, My Brother.*
The only reason to wake up in so poor a place.

Every detail I notice
that others do not see
brings fresh proof
that I am not of this place.
I long for the coolness
of primitive dawn.

I would like to lose
all awareness
of my being
to blend
into nature
and become a leaf,
a cloud
or the yellow of the rainbow.

We piss, my nephew and I,
off the edge of the cliff.
Two continuous streams.
Pure arcs.
A slight smile on both our faces.

I hear a man singing
but do not see his face.
Someone tells us he is crippled
and never leaves his room.
A song so desperate
it has lost all humanity.

The coffee arrives. The taste of Césaire immediately comes into
my mouth. Césaire who spoke of "those who explored neither
the seas nor the sky but those without whom the earth would
not be the earth." Now they are walking past me, in this little
market that's slowly coming to life.

People here are not
in the habit of complaining.
They have the ability to change
all pain into song.
The tobacco the women
chew at noon
shaded by their broad hats
makes the bitter taste of life tolerable.

I slip the old water-warped copy
of *Notebook of a Return to the Native Land*
into my nephew's bag.
We need it before we leave.
Not when we return.

In his own way, he seems very happy with this trip that has
helped him understand the difference between the big city and
peasant life. But I can feel he is beginning to miss his friends
from university and wants to be back in the urban dirt and
violence. That's what he's made of. A person doesn't change his
nature in a few days.

In the end I decide to go ahead on my own. With no other protection than the blood that runs in my veins. I give the rest of my money to Monsieur Jérôme who refuses it at first, but I convince him he will make better use of it than I. Two letters hastily scribbled on the car's burning hood. The longest to my mother and the other to the former minister who willingly let me use his car. A final hug for my nephew and I climb into this shuddering jalopy, with my black hen as sole companion. Destination Baradères, my father's native village.

I watch the Buick 57 pull away in a small cloud of dust as I negotiate the fare with the driver. You were in good company, he tells me with a conspiratorial smile. My nephew and the minister's chauffeur. That's what you think, but I recognized Zaka. Zaka, god of peasants. How did you recognize him? A throaty laugh that signifies the end of the conversation. I find a spot in the back of the truck.

And Now Baradères, My Father's Village

Sacks of green bananas.
Cans of oil.
Coal and flour.
Chickens, goats and even a donkey.
A fat man snoring in the back.
Rumbling breath issuing from the bottom of his belly.

I banish all reflection
even the most intimate
and give in to the embrace of this crowd
where the boundary between man and animal
is so narrow as the truck
makes its way through the arid landscape.

A soft voice behind me. A woman in black whose husband has
just died. The mother and the son lived in Brooklyn, though
the father stayed in Haiti. She tells her story. The first time she
saw him was at the door to the lycée. Her girlfriends made fun
of him. But he was so sweet she immediately fell in love with
him. He was shy, even in their private life, and he remained that
way till the end. He was a delicate man. He died of throat cancer,
without a complaint. His name was Séraphin.

The coffin is at the back. Securely tied to a bench. Taking up
space for six passengers. Since he is dead the widow paid for
four seats only. She wouldn't have had to pay anything if she
had agreed to have the coffin tied to the roof of the truck. She
decided, whatever the price, Séraphin would not ride up there
with the dust and the goats and the chickens. They would make
their last journey together.

His young son is wearing a white shirt
and a black tie.
His head leans on his mother's shoulder.
Somber and silent.
I hear a lady whisper,
"The spitting image of his father."
She knew him well.

Actually, I'm in the same situation.
Except I have no body with me.
And almost no memory of the departed.
This journey is to bring him back
to his village that I will be discovering at the same time.

A funeral without a body.
A ceremony so intimate
it concerns only me.
Father and son, for once,
alone face to face.

To disappear without a trace.
Or anyone to remember you.
Only a god deserves such a destiny.

Here is Baradères in the rain.
It's been raining for two days.
Water rises fast here.
Houses on stilts.
The truck turns carefully behind the church.

We come upon a modest cemetery
under water where small golden fish
swim into the cavities
of freshly buried bodies.

A small group is waiting
at the foot of the tall cross.
Soaked to the skin.
The gravity of death.

The boy in the black tie
is not so sure he wants to get out of the truck.
He doesn't know all these relatives
who have stepped out of another age.
Or this town drowned by the rain.
Or this cemetery where his father will be buried.
In Brooklyn it's hard to imagine Baradères.

In every cemetery there is
a large black cross by the gate.
And an empty grave that belongs to no one.
That's where Baron Samedi lives,
that funereal and dissolute god
who is the guardian of the cemetery where
no one may enter without his permission.

We stroll along the brightly lit streets
of the world's great cities
with our urbane airs and our educated politeness
not knowing that our lives are filled
with secret feelings and sacred songs
we have lost somewhere inside ourselves
and that resurface only at funerals.

We have two lives.
One belongs to us.
The other belongs
to those who have known us
since childhood.

The mother's tongue.
The father's country.
The son's bewildered look
as he discovers in a single day
his own legacy.

They rush the coffin
toward the far end of the cemetery.
Past the last graves with flowers on them.
A few stones this way and that in the tall grass
where fat pink fish swim.
The best spots, by the entrance,
are reserved for those who
have never left Baradères.

This wild kid who wreaks
havoc in Brooklyn
suddenly discovers
his origins
in a lost village.

He bends over to catch bare-handed
a pink fish with an electric charge.
It sends him hopping on one foot.
The fish makes its getaway
to the sound of the laughing crowd.

I stand at the edge of the group
to attend the ceremony,
not wishing to disturb them.
No one seems to notice I am there.
That's what they want me to think.
I have learned how discreet
people are in this part of the world.

A man comes up to me, his formal manner from another era. It would give us great pleasure were you to remain with us afterward, he tells me. Later I learned he had worked for unesco as a translator and after he retired, he returned to live here. The continuous movement between urban and rural worlds strengthens the bonds between culture and agriculture.

The house where the funeral reception takes place stands on the slope of a deforested hill. The kids, along with a few young goats, keep rushing down it. To dry my clothes, I sit by the fire where ears of corn are being smoked in the coals. A little girl in a pretty blue dress and sparkling eyes brings me a cup of coffee. She curtsies by way of greeting. I kiss her on the forehead. She opens her eyes wide then runs off. In a storm of saliva, the retired polyglot confides in me that finally he has time to reread the *Aeneid*.

No one asks me
where I came from nor where I am going.
My past counts no more than my future.
They accept me in the gravity of the present
without demanding explanations.

A starry sky
that makes me dream
of hot evenings on the gallery
with my mother
and of course Baudelaire whose
"The Balcony" was my father's
favorite poem.

I also recall the picnics
Aunt Ninine organized at the beginning of July.
And other precious memories
that convince me, now,
that my childhood was but an
endless season of sunshine,
though the rain did fall.
Nothing is more brilliant than sunlight in the rain.

Suddenly I feel so light.
The sky is no farther
than that banana leaf
that brushes my head.

A Dandy Dies Like a Dandy

I push my way through the banana plantation
divided by a stream
whose song I heard
before discovering in the shadows
its shining back
lit by moonlight.

I come upon an old man
sleeping under a banana tree.
What kind of life
has he lived
to go on smiling
in his dream?

I suppose it was different from
the former minister's who spends his nights
in a museum, where most of the paintings
reproduce the bucolic setting where this peasant is sleeping.
One is living in the other's dream.

I go through the little cemetery.
The earth has drunk up all the water from the sky.
The dead were thirsty
though they do prefer
something stronger.

I just need to look up
to see Sirius
on the collar of Canis Major.
I will spend the night
with this brightest of stars.

I sit down
in the night
on a headstone
to smoke a cigarette.
And think of my father.

That teenager who yesterday was running
nearly naked in the rain
through the streets of Baradères
could have lived out his life
like his friends
who never left their native village.
And never have known
such a strange destiny.

The path trampled through the grass crosses the cemetery and
hits the rocky track that leads to the paved road. He started out
on that path on his way to Port-au-Prince. And years later, to
Havana, Paris, Genoa, Buenos Aires, Berlin, Rome, the world's
great cities. And then New York where I recently saw him stiff
in a black alpaca suit with a magnificent tie of the same color.
Always elegantly dressed. The way his generation was. The only
personal feature: that smile pinned to his face, witness to the
final burst of pain.

My mother questioned me at length
about what he wore for the funeral.
Every detail of his appearance
counted for him—and now for her.
All I remembered were his hands
and his smile.

In the end, once a dandy, always a dandy. Especially when the dandy has stopped taking care of himself. The form can change. The personality, never. If personality never changes, then that Baradères teenager knew everything back then. All the roads he was to take were already laid out inside him.

On a night like this, he must have
looked into the sky at
that great life-size map and seen
all the hospitals, prisons, embassies,
feigned celebrations and lonely nights
that one day he would face.

And if the moon was full and bright
he must have seen my life too,
an extension of his
so similar to it.

We each have our dictator.
For him it was the father, Papa Doc.
For me, the son, Baby Doc.
Exile without return for him.
For me, this enigmatic return.

My father has returned
to his birthplace.
I brought him back.
Not the body
burned to the bone by ice.
But the spirit that made it possible
for him to face
the deepest solitude.

To stand up to that solitude
all those gray days
and cold nights,
how many times did he
picture in his mind
the primitive images
of Baradères in the rain?

He in Baradères.
I in Petit-Goâve.
Then each followed his path
through this wide world.
To return to our point of departure.

He gave me birth.
I take care of his death.
Between birth and death,
we hardly crossed paths.

I have no memory
of my father that I can trust.
That belongs to me alone.
There is no picture
of us alone together.
Except in my mother's memory.

A Son of the Village

Even before the new day dawns
I can hear
the sounds of the town
awakening like a servant girl.
On her tiptoes.

A woman brings me coffee.
The white cup.
The embroidered cloth.
She waits until I have finished drinking it.
The way they say good morning in Baradères.

The man appears soon after. With his hat over his heart.
I make room for him next to me. He sits down. For some time
he says nothing. That's my grave, he murmurs. My whole family
has been buried there for four generations. I immediately get
to my feet. Stay. It's an honor for us. Again this silence I have
no intention of breaking. My wife recognized you. You know
me? Legba. He is confusing me with the god who stands at
the border between the visible and invisible worlds. The one
who allows us to move between them. I've been out of the
country. We know that. I've come to bury my father, and now
I am being welcomed like a god in his native village. We were
waiting for you, he says solemnly. But I am not Legba. You are
the son of Windsor K, my classmate. We went to grammar
school together here. I am amazed, astonished. If we didn't
know who you were, you wouldn't be alive now. You're not the
first to return to bury a family member. I see. But you're the first
I've seen without a body. And you are accompanied by Legba.
And Legba chose to spend the night on our grave. We don't
deserve such an honor. What sign spoke to you of Legba? The

black hen. The hen? Yes, the black hen. Of course, the black
hen. Sometimes you have to pretend to understand, because
here no one will explain to you what you are supposed to know.

A large but skinny and mangy dog
comes and rubs himself against his leg.
I wonder if he
isn't a god too.
The dog star I saw last night.

Children cross the cemetery
on their way to school.
As they go past they run their palm
over their ancestors' graves.
That way they keep daily contact
with the other world.

Last Sleep

By road or by sea?
I choose the sea.
It so happens, the man tells me, there's a sailboat
about to leave the harbor.
It's my cousin Rommel's boat.
A village of cousins.

First we go to La Gonâve for wood
that we'll deliver to Pestel.
Several women get on board the *Epiphany*.
They need oil, salt and flour.
They impose the rhythm of daily life
on the sailboat.

We fish along the way.
On the great salty highway.
Mostly threadfin.
The women never look at the water.
Half the crew doesn't know how to swim.

The sea was off limits to the slave.
From the beach, he could dream of Africa.
And a nostalgic slave
isn't worth much
on a plantation.
He would be killed so his sadness
would not spread to others.

The brilliant sun
in a cloudless sky
and the turquoise sea lined with coconut palms
is just a Northern reverie
for the man trying
to escape the leaden cold of February.

From where I stand I note:
Ferocious beauty.
Eternal summer.
Death under the sun.

We put in at every bay, where various female cousins await the
merchandise in noisy marketplaces. We use the stops to pick
up the necessities of life. New vendors climb aboard, and the
fire in their bodies means they're members of Erzulie Freda
Dahomey's family. The men watch them sleepily. Start something with one of those women and, at the next bay, a new
machete will be waiting in the sun.

Before getting off, a woman wanted to buy my hen to sell it,
she said, at the next market. Just to take it off my hands because
she'd pay market price for it and wouldn't make any profit. The
lady next to me stepped in. Later, she made me swear never to
sell the black hen whatever happened. But I knew that already.

The men are farmers
who work close to their huts.
The women know every one
of the tiny villages where
they sell their vegetables.
Jealous husbands make their wives
stay at the local market.

That gazelle with the slender ankles
accompanies her mother.
Her head down.
A sidelong glance.
She's studying everything
for the day when it's her turn
to make the trip alone.

Up ahead, a small group
of people on the shore.
A sign announces "Les Abricots."
The Indians thought
it was paradise.
I finally get there.

Tall trees whose
branches bend low
to touch the sea.
Big pink fish
still flopping in
the fishermen's boat.
Kids with navels like flowers
devouring perfumed mangos.
The sweet life before Columbus.

I'm not so sure whether
I am in real time
as I move toward
this dreamed landscape.
I've read too many books.
Seen too many paintings.
One day, learn to see things
in their naked beauty.

Always too much hope ahead.
And too much disappointment behind.
Life is a long ribbon
that ceaselessly unfolds
in changing variations
of both.

I go my way
toward a small thatched hut
deep in the banana plantation.
The coffee is prepared
by an Indian princess
with high cheekbones
and the pure breath
of highland women.

In the hammock,
a pre-Columbian invention
that says much
about the degree of refinement
in this society,
you can spend your life
in horizontal meditation.

Three months
to escape the urban intensity
that once gave my life its rhythm.
Three months sleeping
protected by an entire village
that seems to know the source
of that sweet sickness of sleep.

This is not winter.
This is not summer.
This is not the North.
This is not the South.
Life is spherical now.

My former life seems so distant.
That life when I was a journalist, an exile,
a worker, even a writer.
And when I met so many people
for whom now I am no more
than a slowly fading shadow.

Humble houses scattered in the landscape.
Nothing here to recall the Indian genocide
so expertly orchestrated by the Spanish.
His hand on his Alcantara cross
Nicolás de Ovando gave the signal for the massacre
that Arawak memory refuses to forget.

A gentle hand
on my forehead cools my fever.
I doze between dawn and twilight.
And sleep the rest of the time.

Rocked by the music
of the ancient Caribbean wind
I watch the black hen
unearth a worm
that squirms in its beak.
And so I see myself in the jaws of time.

Someone has seen me smile
in my sleep too.
Like the child I was
in the happy times with my grandmother.
A time at long last recovered.
The journey is over.

DANY LAFERRIÈRE is a francophone Haitian and Canadian novelist and journalist. Born in Port-au-Prince, Haiti, and raised in Petit Goâve, Laferrière worked as a journalist in Haiti before moving to Canada in 1976 after the murder of a friend and fellow journalist.

DAVID HOMEL was born and raised in Chicago in 1952 of East European stock. He left at the end of the tumultuous 1960s and lived in Europe and Toronto before moving to Montreal in 1980.

This book is supported by the Institut français
as part of the Burgess programme.

**INSTITUT
FRANÇAIS**

(www.frenchbooknews.com)